# Readers love Andrew Grey

## *A Shared Range*

"…This is one of those stories to read when your heart is bruised and your world feels dark. You'll take a deep breath afterwards and see the sun again."

—Whipped Cream Reviews

## *A Taste of Love*

"…an emotional story that will have you in tears one minute, smiling and laughing the next."

—Love Romances & More

## *Bottled Up*

"…a charming and moving novel."

—Romance Junkies

## *Love Means… No Shame*

"This is one book that will make it to several keeper shelves to be read again and again."

—Literary Nymphs

## *The Best Revenge*

"…this phenomenal story… kept me spell bound from the start."

—Fallen Angel Reviews Recommended Read

**http://www.dreamspinnerpress.com**

Books by
ANDREW GREY

Accompanied by a Waltz
A Taste of Love

THE BOTTLED UP STORIES
Bottled Up
Uncorked
The Best Revenge
An Unexpected Vintage

THE RANGE STORIES
A Shared Range
A Troubled Range

THE CHILDREN OF BACCHUS STORIES
Children of Bacchus
Thursday's Child
Child of Joy

THE LOVE MEANS… STORIES
Love Means… No Shame
Love Means… Courage
Love Means… No Boundaries
Love Means… Freedom
Love Means … No Fear

All published by
DREAMSPINNER PRESS

# A TROUBLED *Range*

## ANDREW GREY

*Dreamspinner Press*

Published by
Dreamspinner Press
4760 Preston Road
Suite 244-149
Frisco, TX 75034
http://www.dreamspinnerpress.com/

A Troubled Range
Copyright © 2011 by Andrew Grey

Cover Art by Reese Dante   http://www.reesedante.com

ISBN: 978-1-61581-829-7

Printed in the United States of America
First Edition
March 2011

eBook edition available
eBook ISBN: 978-1-61581-830-3

# Chapter One

"HAVEN! What in hell are you doing there watching nothin'?" His father's sharp voice carried across the quiet rangeland to where the young man was standing near the gurgling water. "There ain't nothin' over there for you, boy." His father's voice got louder, and Haven turned around, sighing softly before walking away from the fence that formed the border between his family's land and the neighboring ranch. Moving toward his father as the tall man strode across their rangeland toward the small river, Haven stopped himself from taking one last look. "Come on, there's no use lookin', 'cause what's over there don't matter," his dad added sharply, and Haven ducked the halfhearted swipe his dad took at his head.

"I was just looking, wondering why their land looks so much better than ours." Haven made sure he was well away from his father when he said that. If he were close enough, his dad would take another swipe at him, and this time he'd be aiming to hurt.

"You know why. Them fags take more than their fair share of the river and don't leave enough water for us. 'Sides, I won't have you looking and watching them. Whatever Jefferson Holden did wrong with his son, I don't intend to do with you."

Haven fell into stride beside his father. Nearly the man's height and almost as broad, Haven knew he shouldn't have anything to be afraid of when it came to his father. "What makes you think Mr. Holden did anything wrong?"

"You reap what you sow. And Jefferson Holden must have sown something pretty bad to be struck down sick like he was and to have his son turn into some kind of sissy." Kent Jessup turned away from

Haven, spitting out a wad of his chewing tobacco before hauling out the can from his back pocket. "You sure you don't want some?" Kent asked, offering Haven the tin. "It'll make a man out of you."

Haven shook his head, keeping the disgusted look off his face. He'd tried that stuff once and nearly thrown up. Arriving in the yard near the barn, his dad said nothing as he peeled off for the house, and Haven continued on toward the barn. There was plenty to be done. "Don't be shirking your chores," his dad called as he walked up the steps into the house.

"Ain't *me* shirking chores," Haven said under his breath as he walked into the barn. At least it was clean and all the horses were out in their paddocks, not that there were many of the large animals on their ranch. Opening the tack room door, he went inside, grabbing Jake's bridle, checking the leather to make sure it was still sound—something he now did habitually after the reins broke on a set a month ago. Looking around, he saw how old everything looked, and he realized that was because his dad hadn't bought any replacement equipment in years. Even the trucks the ranch lived and died by were almost two decades old.

"Haven, that you?" A deep voice called from outside the door.

"Yeah, Kade, it's me," Haven called as he finished gathering what he needed.

"Thank goodness." Haven heard the relief in the man's voice. He knew that tone well. Everyone on the ranch walked on eggshells around his dad; it wasn't just Haven. "You heading out?"

"Gonna ride fence for the afternoon." It was one of the chores he liked. It got him away from the house for hours, even an entire day at a time. "Need to check the western borders. In the spring, I noticed that some of the posts might be weak, and we'll need to move some of the herd down there in a few weeks, particularly if we don't get any rain." He knew he was testing the fences that bordered the Holden ranch, and if his dad found out, he'd probably be angry as hell for some stupid reason.

"You want me to ride the range, check for any weeds?"

Haven smiled. "Sure. Grab your gear and I'll meet you in the yard, saddled and ready, in half an hour."

Haven watched him go. Kade had energy and a real will to please, and when Haven's dad wasn't around, he did great. Setting his gear on pegs outside the stall, Haven followed Kade outside. He whistled for Jake, and the chestnut gelding came right over, tossing his head excitedly. Taking him by the halter, Haven led his horse into his stall and started the grooming process. Jake loved to be groomed and moved into every stroke of the brush almost like it was a lover. If the big baby had been a cat, he'd have purred.

Slipping the bit into Jake's sensitive mouth, Haven finished saddling the horse, checking the girth twice before leading him out into the yard. "You ready, Kade?"

"Yup," he answered excitedly, climbing into the saddle. They headed out across the range, through the shallow water, before heading west toward the ranch border fence. "Haven."

"Yeah," he answered as he made for the line of fence posts.

"Why's your dad hate Dakota so much? He's never been anything but nice to everybody, far as I know. Helps everybody out when they need it and more than most, from what I hear." Kade didn't look up as he watched the pastureland around him, looking for anything that could make the cattle sick.

"The only thing I can figure is because Dakota's queer." Haven saw Kade's head jerk up at the word. He knew he shouldn't have used it, especially with the feelings he himself had had for as long as he could remember. Haven knew Kade was looking at him and he needed to cover somehow. "Not that it matters to me, but then Dad always held with that church stuff, I never paid it no mind," he added as nonchalantly as he could. Haven made his way toward the fence line, with Kade a little ways away watching the ground. "Maybe it's just 'cause Dad's jealous or something. Everything that happens, he tries to blame it on the Holdens, always has. God himself could sweep down in a blaze of glory, and he'd blame the Holdens that God's brightness hurt his eyes."

Kade snickered, but said nothing more before riding off to continue checking the range. Haven moved closer to the fence, watching the wire and posts as Jake followed the route he knew well. A few of the posts looked as though they might be ready to give, and Haven dismounted, holding Jake's reins as he checked, but they held fine, and he remounted, continuing on his way. In a few places, he saw where posts had already been replaced, and he made a note to thank Dakota the next time he saw him. There was no way he'd tell his dad, who would only yell that Holden had been on his property rather than being grateful that the man had actually fixed the fence for them.

At the far end of the range, Haven looked back along the line before starting down the back section. He saw Kade weaving through the range and let his thoughts wander. He liked it out here alone where he could think, away from his father's stiflingly vocal self-righteous convictions. Fencing and posts passed by as he and Jake slowly made their way along the back of the range. Post after post, acre after acre, passed by them. A few times, he pulled Jake up to check posts and to help keep his eyes sharp.

At the far corner of the range, he dismounted and fished in his saddlebags for pliers. Jake lowered his head, feeding, looking content, as Haven worked to fix a break in the fence. Twisting the barbed wire back together, Haven worked carefully, keeping his gloved fingers away from the barbs, but as he repaired one break, another section of wire pulled away from the post. "Damn it!" Haven swore—there just wasn't quite enough wire left to really fix it. After working awhile, Haven finally managed to knit the break back together.

*Crack!* The sound had Haven jumping out of his skin. Looking around, he saw the dark clouds of a storm rolling in fast from the west. "It's okay, Jake. Let's go home." Haven could feel the horse's nervousness, and he opened the saddlebag to put his tools away. *Crack! Boom!* Thunder rolled through the air, making the ground shake. Jake reared, and Haven found his butt bouncing on the ground as Jake raced away in a complete panic, hooves tearing up the ground as he got smaller and smaller, galloping back toward the barn faster than Haven could ever hope to.

*"Shit!"* Haven hollered as the wind picked up. With nothing else to do, Haven began walking the fence line back the way he had come. If he were lucky, the storm would be dry, bringing wind and noise, but no rain. But he doubted that as the next gust of wind carried the scent of water on it, and he picked up the pace, practically running.

Haven looked around, but knew what he'd see: nothing at all for miles in any direction except open range and fence. There had once been a range cabin just beyond the fence, but it had fallen down in a storm a few years earlier, and his dad was too cheap to rebuild it. So he had no choice. He had to walk and pray. He knew Kade was far away and had hopefully made it back to the ranch.

Another crack was followed instantly by a clap of thunder that had Haven holding his ears and clamping his eyes shut. He swore he could almost feel the heat. He sure as hell could smell the crackling in the air. Looking up, he saw smoke rising from the range just to the west. "Holy fuck," he said to himself, eyes wide in fear, "the range is on fire!" Haven hurried, racing along the fence line as the smoke grew in intensity, spreading in the nearly dry grass.

The first raindrop splatted against his shoulder, big and full, followed by several more. Looking up at the nearly black sky, Haven checked for swirls, but saw none. As he continued to hurry along the fence line, the wind picked up again as the sky opened up, sheets of rain wetting him to the skin in an instant. At least he didn't have to worry about the fire, but the rain picked up even more, buckets of water driven past him by gale-force winds, his wet shirt flapping in the wind.

With no shelter at all, his only choice was to continue trying to get home. Haven knew it wasn't safe out in this weather, but he didn't have a choice.

Finally, he reached the fence corner and began the turn toward the house. He could barely see, the water blowing into his eyes. "Haven."

Hearing his name in the wind, he tried to call back, but just got a mouthful of water. Peering through the gloom, he saw a figure on horseback materialize on the other side of the fence. "Haven, is that you?"

"Yes," he called into the wind as a horse and rider came closer on the other side of the fence. "Dakota?" He couldn't see for sure who it was in the yellow rain gear.

"Climb through the fence." Dakota got off the horse and carefully spread the wire. Haven did the same, gingerly threading himself between the sharp barbs before standing next to the snorting horse. "Get on behind me, and we'll get you inside." Dakota mounted the huge horse before pulling Haven up behind him. Haven held on tight as the horse began to move.

"How can you see in this?"

"I can't, but Roman knows the way, and he'll get us back to the house. Just hang on."

The horse began to move, and Haven closed his eyes, holding on to Dakota, letting the other man's body shield him from at least some of the wind and rain. Periodically, the sky lit up and thunder rocked the air. Haven tensed, expecting the horse to throw them both and bolt, but he didn't. A few times, Haven heard Dakota soothing the horse.

Finally, the wind seemed to stop even as the rain continued sluicing down his back. Moving his eyes away from Dakota, he saw the barn and other buildings, lights casting their rays through the downpour. "Get down and go on inside. If I know Wally, he's looking out the windows worrying himself about both me and you."

Haven slipped off the horse, feet landing in the mud. Dakota dismounted and led the horse into the barn. Looking around at the unfamiliar yard, he made for the light on the front porch. As his foot touched the steps, the front door opened and a slight man stood in the square of light. "Come on in."

"But I'll drip everywhere," Haven said, standing on the porch, dripping all over the wood floor. He recognized the man from town and knew this was Wally, the new vet in the area. He hadn't met him properly yet, but at least he knew who the man was.

"It'll clean," Wally said before backing away, motioning him inside.

As soon as he stepped on the rug, the door closed behind him, and Wally handed him a towel. "Take off your shirt and get yourself dry. I pulled out some dry clothes of Kota's. They might be a little big, but they'll be warm and dry."

Standing in the warm room, Haven pulled off his shirt and began toweling himself off, starting to shiver. When he was outside, he hadn't had time to worry about anything other than getting out of the storm, but now he was cold to the bone. "Thank you."

"It's no trouble," Wally said with a smile. "The bathroom's right down the hall, first door on your left. I set the dry clothes in there for you, and don't worry about dripping, you won't hurt anything."

Haven nodded, clutching the towel around his shoulders as still more thunder rumbled and the lights flickered, but stayed on, thank God.

Padding down the hall, dripping everywhere, Haven found the bathroom and shut the door, stripping out of his soaked clothes and drying himself before pulling on the warm sweats Wally had set out. Finally, he felt warm and dry.

"Just leave your wet things in the tub, and I'll get them in the dryer for you." Wally's voice drifted through the door.

"Okay, thanks," Haven answered, setting the clothes in the tub like Wally asked before drying his hair. He remembered his cell phone in his pocket and fished it out—dead and fried. Stepping out of the bathroom, he padded into the living room as Dakota walked in the front door, minus his rain gear. "You okay?"

"Yes, thanks to you. The storm came up so fast, and then the thunder spooked my horse and he ran off," Haven explained, feeling like a fool for being caught outside like that. "How'd you find me?"

Dakota took off his shoes before stepping the rest of the way in the house. "Wally was out checking Schian, and he saw you riding fence, but he didn't see you return. And when the storm broke, he told me you were probably in trouble." Dakota walked through the room. "Make yourself comfortable. The storm's going to last a while," Dakota said just before disappearing down the hall.

"I'm sorry to be such a bother," Haven told Wally, who was finishing up drying the floor with an old towel.

"It's no bother. By the way, I'm Wally Schumacher. I'd shake hands, but I'm down here," Wally said as he finished cleaning the floor and stood up. "I'm just glad Dakota was able to find you. It's been a while since I saw a storm come up as fast as this one did." Thunder sounded again, this time from farther away.

"I should call my dad to make sure he knows where I am. Kade was out with me too."

"Phone's right on the counter, help yourself."

Haven picked up the receiver and dialed the number. It was answered on the first ring. "Dad, it's me."

"Haven, what happened to you, boy?"

"I'm fine. Jake ran off, and I was stranded on the range. Did Kade get back okay?"

"He and Jake both got back at the same time. I take it you're okay. You know, you could have called sooner. When will you be back? The storm's made a mess, and we'll need to get it cleaned up." Haven noticed the nearly complete lack of fatherly concern, not that he'd come to expect any. It had been a long time since his dad had shown any concern for anything except what he wanted.

"I'll be back once the storm lets up." Without waiting for an answer Haven hung up the phone, glad that both Jake and Kade were okay. The rest could wait until morning. There wasn't much anyone could do about anything now, no matter what his dad said. Once the rain let up, it would be pitch black, anyway.

"Everything okay?" Wally asked as he handed Haven a steaming cup of what he thought was coffee, but with one whiff, the scent of rich hot chocolate filled his senses.

Haven sipped the warm chocolate, sweetness sliding down his throat. "I guess." Haven looked up and saw Dakota coming down the hall pushing an older man in a wheelchair, stopping and positioning him next to the sofa.

"Dad heard voices and wanted to meet our company. Dad"—the older man's head turned slowly—"this is Haven Jessup. Haven, this is my father, Jefferson Holden." Dakota's dad began to tremble and lifted a hand with twisted fingers, shaking it at their guest, and Haven set down the mug, moving away.

"Dad, what are you doing? I know you don't get along with Haven's dad, but you can't take it out on him."

The hand stopped shaking and settled back on the arm rest. "Okay, Kota." Jefferson extended his hand, and at first Haven wasn't sure what to do, but then he realized Jefferson was offering it, so he stepped forward, shaking it carefully.

"I've heard a lot about you," Haven said, and Jefferson made a dismissive sound. Haven released the older man's hand.

"Dad, if you can't behave, I'll take you back to your room. Haven is a guest in our home, and regardless of what's between you and his father, it has nothing to do with him." Dakota walked to the window and looked outside. "The rain's letting up. I can probably take you home whenever you're ready."

Haven finished his hot chocolate and handed the mug back to Wally. "It was nice to meet you, Mr. Holden. I have heard a lot about you from other people in town, good things. I never listen to my father when it comes to other people. I like to make up my own mind." Haven turned to Wally. "Thank you for everything. I'll return the clothes tomorrow."

"You're welcome."

As Haven walked toward the door, he felt a hand brush his arm. "You are welcome here anytime," Dakota's dad said haltingly, and he seemed to smile. Haven smiled back and followed Dakota outside into the wet night and into near chaos.

*Chapter Two*

PHILLIP sat in the car on the side of the road, the rain pelting the roof sounding like stones as huge drops burst on the metal and glass of his vehicle. Claps of thunder shook the car, and a few times, Phillip swore he could see lightning hit just outside his car, light and sound coming at the same time. Windows fogged as he sat and waited for the rain to let up enough that he could make it down the unfamiliar country roads. Picking up his phone from inside the center console in his car, he dialed Dakota and Wally's number, but the damn phone still refused to connect. He'd never seen rain like this before, not even last year when he and Wally had encountered a tornado on their way West. Putting the phone away, he sat back and waited. It was all he could do.

Finally, the rain let up and the rumbles became less frequent, softer and more rolling as opposed to sharp. "Thank God that's over," Phillip said to himself as he started the car, pulling back onto the road. High-beam headlights shone off the water droplets as he inched forward, pavement showing ahead. With the intensity of the storm, Phillip swore he wouldn't have been surprised to find the entire world washed away. Speeding up, Phillip listened carefully to the deep GPS voice as he got closer and closer to his destination. Finally he turned into the long drive that led to the ranch house.

Lights from everywhere shone into his car windows as the wipers scraped over the now almost-dry windshield. Pulling off to the side, Phillip stopped the car and opened the door to get out, stretching his legs as he placed his feet on the ground, entering sheer pandemonium. People raced around, yelling orders. Not a single person noticed him as they hurried between house and barns, saddling horses.

"Dakota," Phillip called as he saw the rancher bound down the front steps. "What's going on?"

"Phillip." Dakota smiled for a fraction of a second. "Sorry about this, but part of the fence came down in the storm, and some of the cattle got out into a neighbor's range, and we need to get them back. Wally's inside, and I'll be back as soon as I can." Dakota hurried away, and Phillip walked up the front stairs, opening the door and stepping inside.

Jefferson sat in the living room, eyes closed. Wally walked down the hall, and seeing Phillip, broke into a huge smile before hurrying up to him and hugging him tight. "You made it," Wally said, releasing him. "When you didn't call, I was starting to get worried."

Phillip slipped off his jacket, and Wally took it, hanging it in the closet. "I waited out the rain on the side of the road and couldn't get a signal because of the storm."

"You want some help bringing in your things?" Wally asked as he walked toward the door. "I have a room all set up for you. You have to be exhausted after the drive."

"Kind of," Phillip answered, as he followed Wally outside into the now-quiet night. Phillip fished for his keys and popped the trunk. "You'll be happy to know I packed light."

Wally reached the back of the car and began to laugh. "This is packing light?" Phillip stood next to his friend, joining in the mirth as they stared at the bursting trunk.

"Well," Phillip started to say, "I got everything in the trunk this time."

"Come on, Suzanne," Wally teased, referencing Suzanne Sugarbaker from *Designing Women*. "Let's get your things inside." Wally tugged on the first suitcase, but it refused to budge. "How'd you even get this in here?"

Phillip just smiled and started removing the other bags, handing them to Wally, who trundled back to the house. Phillip grabbed an armload as well, following his friend inside and down the hall. "Same room as last time?"

"Yeah." Wally opened the door and set his load by the bed before heading out for another. Phillip set down the suitcases he was carrying, looking around the familiar room. The last time he was here, he hadn't used it much, spending a lot of his time with Mario, the sexy and uninhibited ranch foreman.

"This is the last of it," Wally said as he set down the bags on the floor. "How long are you planning to stay?" Wally asked, and Phillip noticed him looking at the bags covering almost every inch of floor.

"I don't know. I got laid off two weeks ago and thought I'd take a break before starting the job-hunting process. Damned recession, but what can you do? At least I have savings, so I won't be out on the street." He was counting the blessings he had. The layoff had hit him hard, not that he wanted anyone else to know it had. The only thing keeping him going was looking forward to this time away… and maybe Mario? As Phillip looked into Wally's eyes, he knew his friend understood, probably too much.

"You're welcome here for as long as you want to stay." Wally sat on the edge of the bed as Phillip began unpacking. "Was the drive out okay?"

Phillip smiled like the smartass he was. "Except for nearly being washed off the road, yes."

"No tornados?" Wally asked with a grin.

"No, I did not have to pull under any freeway overpasses, huddling with strangers as we prayed for our lives, thank you very much. Instead I got to pray that God wouldn't come out of heaven and tell me to start building an ark." Wally laughed and Phillip joined him. It felt good to laugh again; he hadn't done much of that lately. "When I arrived, I didn't see Mario," Phillip said in what he hoped was a casual manner, even though he'd have been lying to himself if he didn't admit he was excited about the prospect of seeing him again. Wally turned, and the look on his face told Phillip everything he needed to know. "Oh, how long has he been gone?"

Wally narrowed his eyebrows. "Mario isn't gone." Phillip relaxed. He must have misread Wally's expression. "But he and David have been seeing each other for the last...." Wally drew out the last word as he thought. "I guess six months or so."

Phillip sat on the edge of the bed, feeling the way he had the day his boss had told him his services weren't needed anymore. Not that he put it that way, but the insincere bastard might as well have. All fake smiles and simulated sympathy. "Oh, I guess I should have known." Phillip sighed as he got up and began putting his things away, wondering how he was going to feel when he saw Mario again. "What does this David do?"

"He's one of the hands Dakota hired about eight months ago when he began expanding the herd." He heard the bedsprings creak as Wally got to his feet. "I know you feel bad, but don't let it get you down. You and Mario were casual, and you said yourself that it was just a bit of fun, anyway."

"I know." Phillip turned away from the suitcase he'd opened to look at Wally. "I'm twenty-eight, unemployed, and alone. I know it's my own fault, but it doesn't make me feel any better." He lifted out a stack of underwear, laying it in a drawer. "I guess I was hoping I might find out there was something more." Phillip kept unpacking. "I'm just feeling sorry for myself right now. What I probably need is a good night's sleep."

"Well, I'll leave you, then. You know where things are, and I laid out towels for you in the bathroom." Wally turned to leave. "If you hear us in the night, don't worry. I sometimes have to leave on calls. Dang horses always give birth in the middle of the night," Wally said as he winked at him before leaving, closing the door behind him.

Phillip finished unpacking, putting his suitcases and bags in the bottom of the closet. He thought about just going to bed, but changed into sweats and walked out to the living room. Jefferson still sat alone, watching television, eyes open and bright. "When did you get here?" Jefferson asked, his voice soft, words slightly slurred but very understandable.

"About an hour ago," Phillip answered, taking a seat on the sofa next to the wheelchair. "Who's winning?" Phillip asked, not really caring about baseball, but he remembered from his last visit that Dakota's dad was a real fan.

"Don't know, just woke up. Are the boys still out?"

"Wally's in bed, I think, and Dakota's out with the men trying to fix some fence that blew down in the storm. Hopefully they'll be back soon. Do you need to go back to your room?"

"No, just wondering," Jefferson answered softly. "You wanna beer?"

Phillip chuckled. "Sure, I'll have one if you will." He knew that was exactly what the man was angling for. Phillip stood up and walked into the kitchen, opening the refrigerator door. He snagged two beers, and after twisting off the tops, he walked back into the living room, placing one of the bottles in Jefferson's twisted hand. Once he was sure Jefferson had a grip on it, he sat back down, watching the game and drinking the beer. Every once in a while, Jefferson would grunt or make some sound. At first, Phillip thought something might be wrong, but he quickly learned it was the older man reacting to the game.

Phillip fell into a sort of dazed, half awake, half asleep feeling as the beer relaxed him, so he jumped slightly when the front door opened and Dakota stepped inside. "Hey, Dad," Dakota said as he took off his jacket. "I see you conned Phillip out of another beer."

Phillip got up and walked to his friend, receiving a hug, surprised when Dakota was followed in by a younger man, almost as broad and tall. Turning, Dakota spoke to the stranger. "Haven, I'll give you a ride home as soon as I get my dad to bed." Dakota looked at Phillip. "You gonna be up for a while?"

"Sure. Wally went to bed a while ago, but I can stay up for a bit," Phillip answered, noticing that the other man kept looking at him.

Phillip knew that look—one of confused desire that closeted boys got when they saw something that they were attracted to, but weren't sure if they wanted to kiss or kill. Phillip saw Dakota take the nearly full beer bottle from his dad before wheeling him away down the hall toward his bedroom. The kid, Dakota had said his name was Haven, sat on the far edge of the sofa. "I'm Phillip, Phillip Reardon. Do you work for Dakota?"

Haven shook his head. "Haven Jessop. My dad's ranch is just to the east of Dakota's place." He seemed nervous and uncomfortable, but Phillip felt confident that he wasn't the source. There seemed to be something else that had the man wound as tight as a drum.

"Did you get the fence fixed?"

"Yes," Haven answered, and he seemed to wind himself even tighter. Leg bouncing on the floor, eyes darting around the room, Haven almost seemed as though he was ready to explode at any minute. Dakota's footsteps in the hall seemed to trigger him, and Haven jumped to his feet as Dakota entered the room. "That section of fence was fine this afternoon," he blurted out excitedly, like he'd been waiting hours to say something.

"It couldn't have been. The post was rotten."

Haven stepped closer, looking earnestly at Dakota. "I know it looked rotten, which is why I checked it by hand. I saw it when I was on Jake and tested it. The post looked bad, but it didn't budge when I tugged on it." Haven was speaking louder, and Dakota looked dubious. Footsteps in the hall silenced everyone.

"Kota," Wally said from the hallway, "you're being an ass. I can tell from here that he's telling the truth, and since when do we call people liars who just spent two hours helping us fix fences and get our cattle back in their ranges?"

Phillip had never seen the wind fly out of Dakota's sails so fast before, but Wally wasn't done. "I believe Haven's telling the truth, and I think you should have a better look at the post tomorrow morning, when you can see. In the meantime, he needs to go home before his father has some sort of conniption, and you need to come to bed." Without another word, Wally turned back down the hall.

"Let me take you home," Dakota said to Haven.

"I'll do it, Dakota. You go on to bed. You're dead on your feet." Phillip walked toward his room. "I'll put on some shoes." Phillip went to his room and slipped on some sneakers. When he returned, the two men were talking quietly and most of the tension had thankfully dissipated. "You ready to go?" Phillip asked, and Haven nodded, as Dakota covered a yawn with his hand.

"I promise I'll check the post in the morning. I had the men throw it in the back of the truck."

"Thanks," Haven replied with a slight smile before following Phillip outside and across the yard to his car. "My dad's gonna blow a gasket. I was supposed to be home hours ago," Haven said just before Phillip started the engine.

Phillip put the car in gear and pulled down the drive. "Just say you were helping Dakota out. He should understand. Doesn't everybody help everyone else out around here?"

Haven had him turn left. "My dad and Dakota's dad have been enemies for years. Don't know why, but if my dad finds out I was at the Holden ranch, he'll skin me alive. It's been that way ever since I could remember." Haven pointed out the window. "The drive's just up on the left about another half mile."

Phillip watched for the drive and turned, pulling up to the small house, stopping the car. "I'll see you around, and I promise not to tell your dad where you were."

Haven smiled, his face warming, eyes sparkling with a touch of happiness. "Thanks, I appreciate that." Haven opened the door and climbed out of the car. "I'll see you around."

The door closed, and Phillip watched as Haven climbed the steps to the house, disappearing inside. Phillip turned his car around and headed back down the drive toward the ranch.

Parking out of the way, Phillip got out of the car, surprisingly not at all sleepy. He looked toward the foreman's cabin, its windows dark, thinking of Mario and the times he'd spent in that cozy little house with Mario keeping him warm. Wally was right. It had been foolish and unfair of him to think Mario would be waiting for him to come back. Truthfully, Phillip had started to wonder if he was made to settle down, but the bouts of loneliness were becoming more frequent, and he found himself becoming more and more jealous of the couples he seemed to be spending time with. Phillip smiled as he could almost hear Wally's voice asking him what it was he wanted. He'd always thought he'd fall for a huge guy with muscles and strength, both inside and out.

Without thinking, Phillip found himself wandering into the barn, a small light at the far end enough for him to see the large heads poking out of the stalls to see what was going on. "It's okay, guys, didn't mean to disturb you," Phillip told the horses before turning around. Leaving the barn, he wandered toward the front porch and into the house. Tired or not, he wasn't going to sort his life out in a few minutes.

Opening the door quietly, he lightly stepped through the nearly dark house, making his way toward the bedroom. Cleaning up as softly as he could, Phillip slid beneath the crisp sheets and did his best to let the worries and cares that seemed to follow him lately fall away. Once he relaxed, Phillip smiled as he thought of Haven and the warmth in the brief smile he'd seen and the earnest way he'd needed Dakota to believe him. The boy was cute, he had to give him that.

Yawning widely, Phillip rolled over, bunching the pillow under his head. That was enough. Morning would come early, and if he knew Wally, the man would have him up at the ass-crack of dawn. It would almost be worth it if Haven would be there, too, but he wasn't holding much hope of actually seeing the man again. Rolling over, Phillip closed his eyes and remembered nothing else till morning.

## Chapter Three

THE shovel scraped the concrete floor as Haven worked in the barn cleaning one of the stalls. This was usually one of Kade's chores, but Haven needed something to do, and he also figured he needed to apologize to the man. Not that he'd really done anything wrong, but he knew Kade had worried about him. Besides, right now, the last person he wanted to see was his father, and if he was doing the dirty work, the chances were his dad would be as far away as he could get. Throwing the soiled bedding onto the wheelbarrow, Haven rested the blade on the floor, leaning against the handle, thinking.

He'd been lucky. It had rained like cats and dogs and the wind had blown things around, but luckily they'd escaped without much damage. Haven tried to think why his dad had told him things were a mess, because he'd been up for a few hours and already things were back to normal. Haven heard the door open and went back to work until he recognized Kade's footsteps. "Are the herds okay?"

"They're fine, eating grass like nothing happened," Kade said as he appeared in the stall doorway. "You don't have to do that."

"It's okay. If you want to help, there's one more, and we'll be done in here. I'm leaving the horses in the paddocks today. They're surprisingly sound after all that rain, and it'll do the horses good to be outside." The rain seemed to have ushered in some cooler weather that would do the entire ranch some good. They didn't get many days like this through the summer, nice temperatures and clear skies, and when they did, the entire ranch seemed to revel in it.

"I'll clean Jake's stall and then make sure everything's shipshape. I sort of want to check the barn roof up close to make sure there wasn't any damage. It's pretty old, and it wouldn't do to have the hay get wet."

"I'll help you when we're done here," Haven added as he returned to work. "That roof will be hot as hell if we wait too long."

"Yeah, I know it," Kade said, and a few seconds later Haven heard the sound of the other stall door opening and then the scraping of the shovel. They worked in silence, concentrating on their tasks until both stalls were clean and fresh bedding spread. Putting their tools away, Haven helped Kade get out the tall ladder, and they leaned it against the side of the barn and climbed to the roof. "You don't have to come up here if you don't want to, Haven," Kade called down as Haven stood at the base of the ladder, looking up toward the roof. "I know you hate heights." Kade's head disappeared, and Haven girded his loins and climbed the ladder.

"How does it look?" he asked, reaching the edge of the roof, peering up at Kade, who wandered over the sloped surface like it was nothing at all.

"Pretty good, actually. Doesn't appear to be any damage, although there're a few spots that'll need some repair, but I don't think they're from the storm." Kade made his way back over to the ladder. "Haven, I'm sorry about yesterday."

"What for?"

"I left you on the range during the storm. You're my best friend, and I left you alone."

"You did what you were supposed to do. You saw the storm coming and headed in. You had no way of knowing that I wasn't paying attention."

"What happened, anyway? Where'd you find shelter?" Kade asked as he moved closer, and Haven began climbing down, testing each rung with his foot before placing weight on it, feeling relieved as he saw the ground coming closer. On the ground, he waited for Kade.

"I got stuck on the far edge, and Dakota found me and took me back to his place." Haven looked around to make sure his dad was nowhere in sight. "They were really nice to me. Why my dad hates them so much is beyond me, but I know it's mutual. I met Dakota's dad, and there's definitely no love on that side, either."

"Don't let your dad find out, or he'll skin you alive."

"Haven! Where are you, boy?"

"Speak of the devil," Haven said, turning around to see his father striding across the yard. "Check on the horses and make sure they have enough fresh water and hay," Haven told Kade, and the hand moved to get started.

"When did you get in?" his dad asked as he approached.

"Once the storm ended, a friend drove me home." He knew he had to stop his dad from asking too many questions. "I already checked things out, and there doesn't seem to be any permanent damage. Just some stuff that got blown around, but that's already cleaned up."

"I want you to open the gates and fill the retention ponds while the water's high. It'll go down just as fast as it came up if we don't get more rain."

"I know. I was planning to do that this afternoon." The ponds were close to Holden land, and he figured he could go over and ask about that fence post.

"See that you do. I'm headed into town to pick up the supply order. I'll be back later." His dad strode away, and Haven shook his head. Whenever his dad went for the supply order, a two-hour task took all day because his dad would spend hours with his cronies in one of the local watering holes, but at least Haven would have a chance to get away.

"I'll see you then," Haven said to his father's back, and he went back to work, listening for the sound of truck tires on the driveway signaling his dad was gone.

After finishing his chores for the morning and making sure the hands all had their tasks for the day, Haven made a couple of quick sandwiches, which he ate in a hurry before saddling Jake to go check the water retention ponds.

The rangeland smelled clean, fresh, like it only did just after a good rain. As he rode, the air was crisp, he could almost sense new growth that the rain would bring. The sound of water reached his ears before he saw the rushing current the river had risen to overnight. Riding to the bridge, he and Jake crossed it before riding to the old gate. Haven checked that it was still solid before walking the length of the small canal to where the pond water sparkled in the sun, a ring around it, much higher than the water, showing where the water had once been.

Haven's grandfather had dug the pond years earlier, and even though it needed to be dredged deeper, everything looked in order, and Haven walked back, turning the valve that started the water flowing down the canal. Faster and faster it flowed, filling the canal. It would take hours, even days, for the pond to fill, and Haven hoped the water stayed high enough to do just that.

"Haven." He heard someone call, the voice carried on the wind, and he looked around, seeing a man on the other side of the border fence, waving to him with one hand. He returned the wave, unsure of who it was at this distance.

Making a check that all was well, water flowing cleanly into the pond, he mounted Jake and rode toward the figure. As he approached, Haven recognized the man who'd given him the ride home. "What are you doing out here without a horse?" Haven asked as he approached.

"I have one, of sorts," Phillip said with a grin, pointing to the ATV a little ways away. "I came out to give Dakota a hand with the permanent fence repairs, but it seems I'm not much help." Phillip smiled brightly, the sun sparkling in his eyes. "That's not really true. I'm no help at all." Phillip laughed warmly at his own joke.

"Then why do you work for him?" Haven asked as he swung down on his side of the fence.

"I don't. I met Dakota on a cruise almost two years ago now, and we became friends. Last summer Wally and I came out for a visit. The two lovebirds fell in love, and I came out to visit them when I found myself between jobs."

"Oh." Haven found himself staring at the man, not quite able to figure out what to make of him. "So you're queer like Dakota?"

"Gay," Phillip corrected, "and yes, I am." Phillip's gaze narrowed, and Haven found himself squirming as he turned to look over the range, anywhere but at those eyes that seemed to see inside him. He'd seen that same look the night before, and it had made him just as uncomfortable then. Letting his gaze return, he found those eyes looking at him, watching him, and Haven began to squirm, but stopped himself. He was no wilting flower.

"Where's Dakota now?"

Phillip pointed out over the range that seemed to go on for miles. "Working on the break. Come on, I'll meet you there." Phillip walked toward the four-wheeler, and Haven mounted Jake, riding toward the break in the fence.

Phillip was already there when Haven trotted Jake up to where Dakota was working to splice the wire together. "Hey, Haven, how are things? Did you have any damage at your place?" Dakota asked as Haven walked up to where he was working.

"None other than this fence. I appreciate you fixing it."

Dakota looked up at him, a dark look on his face, though it faded quickly. "I know how our fathers feel about one another, but that doesn't mean we have to. This fence is both of ours and the only thing keeping our herds apart. Besides, helping out is the neighborly thing to do."

"I do appreciate it." Haven looked around when he felt that uncomfortable feeling in his stomach again. "Did you look at the post?"

"Yeah, I did." Dakota set down his tools, standing to his full height. Damn, he was handsome, and Haven reminded himself that he wasn't supposed to be having these feelings for another man, and especially not the neighbor his father hated, and who, not incidentally, was already taken by one of the nicest men he'd ever met. "And you were right. It looked bad, but the inside was solid as a rock."

Haven felt his insides ease somewhat. All night he'd questioned himself whether he'd been right. "So how'd it come down?"

"I wish I knew. Maybe one of the herd broke it off. You know they'll sometimes spook in a storm. But it looked to me like it was cut partway through." Dakota's eyes narrowed.

"I didn't do it," Haven said quickly, backing away, looking at Phillip for support.

"I didn't say you did, and I could be wrong. When I'm done here, you're welcome to come back with us and take a look for yourself. Maybe you can make something out of it." Dakota looked to Phillip. "Can you give me a hand?"

"I can help," Haven offered, "just let me move Jake to your side of the fence."

Dakota nodded his head, and after leading Jake through the break in the fence, Haven took the gloves from Phillip, slipping them onto his hands, holding the wire steady while Dakota clipped off the hanging ends before stringing a new section of wire between the posts around the replacement. They worked quietly, each knowing what to do. The entire time, Haven felt Phillip's eyes on him.

Once they were done, Dakota packed up the tools, cranking up his own four-wheeler and starting toward the house, with Haven and Jake following behind, and Phillip bringing up the rear.

Haven rode into the ranch yard, dismounting, and Wally hurried out of the house, racing to one of the trucks. "Kota, I'm on a call. Hey, Haven." He waved before disappearing into the truck and speeding down the driveway.

"I'll take your horse into the barn," one of the younger men said to Haven, leading Jake away.

"The post is this way," Dakota told him, and he led Haven around the side of the barn, kneeling down to examine the piece of wood lying on the ground. "See what I mean?" He pointed toward one end. "It looks like it was cut partway through."

Haven looked to where Dakota pointed, seeing where the break in the wood appeared flat and suspiciously regular. "It certainly does. But why would anyone want to do that? It makes no sense."

"To me, either, but it looks like someone did just that, and it was sheer luck on our part that one of my men noticed the break, or we'd have spent days driving the escapees back into the range. As it was, it took us hours to round them up." Dakota's quizzical gaze seemed to be asking the same question that Haven asked himself.

"The only one who might benefit would be my dad," Haven reluctantly admitted. "If you failed to round up any of your herd, they'd meld into ours when we moved them into that area. We'd find them eventually, and I'd like to think he'd call you when he discovered it, but...." Haven bit his lower lip, realizing his dad would probably let his hate guide him instead of doing what was right.

"Don't worry, Haven. I know if you discovered it, you'd see to it we got them back," Dakota said as he got to his feet and walked away, leaving Haven alone with the post and his worry.

"You okay?" A hand touched his shoulder, and Haven turned his head, looking right into Phillip's chocolate brown eyes.

"Yeah," Haven said, looking back at the chunk of wood before returning his gaze to Phillip. "Why do you keep looking at me like that?"

"Like what?" Phillip asked, kneeling next to him.

"Like that. Like you can see something you shouldn't be seeing." Haven felt the quiver inside his stomach start again.

"Or something you don't want anyone seeing," Phillip corrected as his gaze drilled into the rancher. "Haven, I've seen that look before, and I know what you're feeling. The quivering in your stomach, the flutter of excitement combined with fear and maybe a touch of shame." Haven couldn't stop himself from nodding before looking away. Phillip had the shame part down, all right.

"How do I make it stop?" Haven asked very softly, barely vocalizing his thought.

A finger touched his chin, and Haven jerked slightly. "Be honest with yourself about what you want. That feeling comes from your fear of who you are and who you want to be with."

"But it's wrong," Haven protested feebly. With Phillip so close, he could barely think at all.

Fingers lightly touched his cheek. "No, it's not. Being honest with yourself about who you are isn't wrong. Your dad probably filled your head with all that crap because he doesn't like it, but that doesn't mean it's wrong. It's just part of who you are."

"Are you saying I'm gay?" Haven asked, looking expectantly into Phillip's eyes, hoping he had the answers to questions Haven had been asking himself for years.

"Haven." Phillip's voice sounded warm and encouraging. "Only you can answer that, but ask yourself this, is it the thought of girls that gets you excited, or a strong, handsome man? There's nothing wrong with either answer. The only right one is the truth."

Haven didn't know what to say and looked away, his emotions conflicted on so many levels. Swallowing hard, Haven asked, "If I'm gay, will I start talking funny and wearing women's shoes?"

Phillip laughed deeply. "Not unless you want to." Phillip moved closer. "Dakota and Wally are gay, and they never wear women's shoes."

"Do you?" Haven asked, feeling a smile threaten.

"Only on Halloween when I get out my Marilyn Monroe outfit," Phillip retorted with a smile, before explaining, "Being gay isn't about what you wear or how you act. It's about who you love." Phillip added softly, moving a little closer still, "The rest is everyone else's problem."

Haven could feel the heat from Phillip's body, the man's scent—sweat mixed with the range and fresh air—reached his nose, and Haven felt his heart race. *Was Phillip going to kiss him? Would he kiss back?* A hand touched his neck, bringing their heads closer together. Haven held his breath, waiting, his heart beating in his chest, swallowing before parting his lips.

The first touch of another man's lips to his surprised him, and Haven almost pulled back, but the sensation deepened, the lips sliding gently against his, Phillip's tongue lightly tracing his. Haven found himself moaning slightly, and the kiss deepened as Phillip cupped his head, intensifying the kiss.

"You know, you two should probably do that someplace where everyone can't see you."

Haven pulled back, falling onto his butt, looking up at Dakota, who smiled back at him. Haven tried to figure out how he could disappear into the ground; he was so embarrassed and ashamed. "I should go." Haven scrambled to his feet, hurrying toward the barn. He'd never felt so humiliated in his life, and he berated himself as he hurried inside looking for Jake.

"Haven, it's okay," he heard Phillip say from behind him. "You didn't do anything wrong. Dakota was just teasing." Phillip touched his shoulder, and Haven shrugged it off. "It really is okay, Haven."

He knew Phillip was trying to be reassuring, but all he wanted was to get away. Finding Jake still saddled, he led the horse out of the barn. Mounting, he took a final look around, seeing Phillip standing in the barn door, before urging Jake toward home.

## Chapter Four

PHILLIP saw Haven ride away and took off running across the yard, catching him as he rode down the street. "Haven, stop, please." Phillip waved his arms and breathed a sigh of relief when Haven pulled his horse to a stop. "Don't leave like this. Dakota was just kidding." Haven looked like a scared rabbit. "You didn't do anything wrong, honest."

"I know," Haven said, but the look on his face was not convincing in the least. "I have to get home before my dad finds out I was here."

Phillip stepped closer, looking up at Haven still sitting on the horse. "Would you have dinner with me?"

"Dinner?" Haven repeated as though he didn't understand.

"Yeah, dinner. You know where we go to a restaurant and eat together, talk a little." Phillip smiled. "I promise not to kiss you in front of everyone. So how about it?"

Haven looked as though he was about to say no and race for home. "Okay, but I'll have to meet you there."

"Tonight at seven. I'm not sure what's in town. It's been a while. But I'd like to take you to a nice place. Is there a steakhouse?"

"You mean like Louie's?" Haven asked.

"Sure, tonight at seven."

Haven began looking around again. "Uh, okay. I'll meet you there at seven."

Phillip stood back, and Haven urged his horse forward. Phillip watched the man's butt move in the saddle for a while before turning around and heading back toward the ranch house. "That wasn't very nice," Phillip said as he stopped near one of the paddock fences, standing next to Dakota.

"I'm sorry. The way he was kissing you, I...." Dakota shook his head as he went back to watching the boys practice whatever rodeo-type thing it was they did with their rope. Phillip had no clue, but found himself watching a man as he threw a lasso around a calf.

"He's a nice kid, and I think that was his first kiss," Phillip said, his finger reaching for his still tingling lips.

"Sorry, but anyone could have seen him, and by anyone I mean his father. The man's a confirmed and certifiable hater of everyone and everything." Dakota turned to look at him. "He would go ballistic if he saw you kissing his son." Dakota's serious gaze made Phillip squirm slightly. "If you're looking for someone to have a little fun with, Haven Jessup is not that person."

Phillip felt the fun and excitement from a few minutes earlier drain away. *Was he only looking for a little fun?* It's what he was usually after, but this time he wasn't quite so sure. Just playing around with Haven didn't seem right. "I don't think I want to, but I'm not sure how to do anything else."

Dakota's eyes widened like he didn't believe him at first. "Just follow your heart, Phillip. Wally would give you all kinds of advice, and you're free to ask him, but that's what I did and it worked for me." Dakota turned back to what was happening in the paddock. "Great ride, David!" he called. A few seconds later, Mario rushed out, grabbing the man around the waist, swinging him around as they celebrated his run. Phillip felt a momentary twinge of jealously, but to his surprise it wasn't because David and Mario were together. Instead he found he was jealous because they had each other. All the guys he'd been with had found someone else: Mario, Dakota, and God knows how many of the other guys he'd been with had found someone, but none of them ever seemed to choose him.

"I asked him to dinner," Phillip said softly, "and he said yes." That pleased him immensely. Oh, he was still worried about seeing someone in the process of coming out, but anyone he met here in Wyoming had to be careful, so Phillip figured it went with the territory.

"Are you sure this is what you should be doing?" Dakota asked, keeping his voice low. "You're going to be leaving when you decide you've had enough of the country life and the city calls to you."

Phillip glared back at Dakota, softening his expression when he saw concern as opposed to condemnation. "He's different," Phillip said, feeling as though he had to explain. "At least I hope this is different."

Dakota smiled slightly. "You're a great guy, Phillip, and I've always thought that once you decided to settle down, you'd find a really great guy too." Dakota's hand squeezed his shoulder as his attention returned to the paddock.

Phillip watched the roping for a while before wandering away. Unsure of where he was going, he found himself drifting behind the house and back toward a fenced-in area near some scrubby trees. As he approached the enclosure, he saw a lion walk toward him, mouth opening in a yawn. "You must be Schian," Phillip commented, staying well back from the fence as big cat eyes blinked at him. Sitting in the grass, Phillip stared at the lion, letting his thoughts wander.

"I see you've met." Wally's voice pulled him out of his thoughts. Turning, Phillip saw Wally standing next to him.

"I wasn't expecting you back for a while," Phillip said as he returned his gaze to the huge cat.

"False alarm. The horse wasn't ready to deliver. She was just looking for a little sympathy." Wally sat next to him in the grass. "He's something, isn't he?" Wally asked, tilting his head toward the lion, who was now pacing the perimeter of the enclosure.

"Yes, but don't you feel afraid with him around? I mean, what if he gets out?"

"He's old, has arthritis, and hip problems. He likes to go for walks, though."

"You take the lion for walks? What do you do, put him on a leash?" The image was almost too much.

"No, but I do open up the second enclosure so he has more room. I wish I could let him out for more. I doubt he'd hurt me, but I can't speak for what could happen if something spooks him. He may have spent most of his life with the circus, but he's still a wild animal."

"Then why is he here?" Phillip asked, keeping an eye on the lion, because he swore he kept seeing the animal licking his lips like Phillip was dinner.

"To live out his life in peace—the circus was going to put him down," Wally said, and Phillip understood, knowing that Wally could never let that happen, not if he could help it. Every animal had a friend in Wally, that was for sure.

"What are the other enclosures for?" Phillip gestured to another set of cages a hundred or so yards away.

"Well, I've decided to open a full-fledged wild animal rescue. The enclosures around Schian are for other carnivores and cats, while those over there are for other kinds of animals. So many people get exotic animals as pets when they're young, and aren't able to care for them properly when the animals reach full size. I do draw the line at snakes and reptiles, though." Wally smiled. "So enough about me, what's going on with you?"

"I have a date with Haven tonight for dinner." Phillip noticed the look on Wally's face. "Before you say it, Dakota's already given me the lecture."

"Do you like him?"

"Yeah. I don't know if he's ready for anything, and if he's not, that's all right, you know?" Phillip didn't quite understand what he was feeling, but he figured going a little slow would be good for both of them.

"When was the last time you went to dinner with a guy without expectations of ending up in bed?" Wally tilted his head slightly, like he was about ready to burst or something. "You can't remember, can you?" Phillip had to admit that he couldn't and shook his head. Wally stood up and extended his hand, pulling Phillip to his feet. "Let's go in and decide what you're wearing on your date."

"It's not until this evening," Phillip replied, slipping his arm around his friend's shoulders.

"Then we'll have just enough time to get you ready," Wally teased as they walked back toward the house.

PHILLIP took a last look in the mirror before grabbing a light jacket. The house seemed quiet, and Phillip listened, hearing what he thought might be a television. Following the sound, he walked to Jefferson's door. Knocking softly, he waited, and the door opened. Jefferson lay on his bed, the baseball game on. A small sofa had been added to the room, and Wally was sitting on it, waiting for Dakota to sit back down. Dakota stepped away from the door, and Phillip followed him inside.

Jefferson made what sounded like a whistling noise. "Going fancy?" he said with his characteristic half smile.

"I'm having dinner with a friend," Phillip said, and Jefferson's eyes twinkled.

"Young man," Jefferson said surprisingly clearly, "I know the difference between going out with friends and going on a date. Those are definitely date jeans."

"You look good," Wally added as he fished for his keys, handing them to Phillip. "Have fun."

"I can take my own car," Phillip told Wally, about to throw the keys back.

"Out here, you need something reliable, and that thing you're driving looks like it's on its last legs, and the roads out here will be the death of it," Wally told him with a slight wink, telling him it was Wally's way of helping him make a good impression.

"Thanks, I think," Phillip said before saying goodnight to everyone as Dakota resettled on the sofa, holding Wally close. Closing the door behind him, he walked through the house and outside to Wally's truck.

The drive to town didn't take long, and it wasn't hard for him to find the steakhouse. He gave his name to the server once he was inside and sat in the waiting area, watching the door. Checking his watch every few minutes, Phillip felt his knee begin to shake. At ten minutes after seven, Phillip got up, ready to leave, just as his name was called. Figuring he'd been stood up, Phillip decided he might as well eat and followed the hostess to the table.

Phillip sat down, and the server approached. "Will you be meeting someone?"

Phillip looked toward the door, shaking his head. "I guess not. But you may as well leave it." He took the offered menu and began looking it over.

"Phillip?" The chair across from his moved, and he lowered the menu. "Sorry I'm late," Haven said softly. "It took me longer than I expected to get away."

Phillip smiled. "I'm glad you're here. I thought you weren't coming."

"I almost didn't." Haven swallowed and took a drink from his water glass. "My dad's been on a tear since I got home, asking where I've been, and then tonight he kept grilling me about where I was going."

"I'm sorry." Phillip set down his menu. "Maybe this wasn't such a good idea. I don't want to get you in trouble." He really didn't.

"It's not you. Dad would pop a vein if he knew I was on a date with another guy. On top of that, he just refuses to see me as anything but a kid, even though I do most of the work around the ranch."

"It's hard for parents to see their kids as adults."

Haven shook his head, but said nothing more as the waiter returned. "Haven," the young man said, smiling.

"Hi, Frankie, how are you?" Haven said to the server, shaking his hand. "It's been a while. You still at UW in Cheyenne?"

"Yeah. It's going well." The server looked to Phillip.

"Phillip, this is Frankie. We went to high school together. Frankie, this is Phillip. He's in town visiting some friends, and I had to bring him here."

Frankie extended his hand, and Phillip shook it. "I'd like to talk more, but my boss is a hardass." Frankie smiled and took their drink orders before hurrying away.

"He seems nice," Phillip commented as he sat back down.

"He is. The guy was the quarterback of our football team, really talented. He got an athletic scholarship and had to turn it down," Haven explained, and Phillip felt his eyebrows raise in surprise. "He got injured before he could play his first game and decided not to push it. Now he concentrates on his studies rather than football."

"Smart kid," Phillip commented.

"He always was. So what do you do?"

"I'm an accountant, but I'm sort of between jobs right now. My company downsized me out of a position. I'd already planned to come out for a visit, but when I get back, I'll have to start looking for another job. Did you always want to be a rancher?"

Haven laughed softly, his face lighting in a bright smile that Phillip found absolutely endearing and incredibly sexy. "No. I wanted to be a fireman, but that really isn't much of an option around here. So I help run the family ranch." Frankie returned with their drinks and took their dinner orders.

"From what you said, you do it all."

Haven nodded slowly, sipping his beer. "Since my mom left when I was a kid, Dad hasn't been the same, I guess. He used to work really hard all the time, but now he just seems to wait for me to do everything."

"Must get tiring," Phillip said, watching the man's expressive eyes.

"It can be, but I really love it, and someday the ranch will be mine. At least I hope so."

Phillip could sense excitement in Haven's voice. "What do you do for fun?"

"Not too much. The ranch takes most of my time. Sometimes Kade and I go into town to take in a movie, or go riding, but mostly I work." Haven took another gulp of his beer. "Kade's one of the hands on the ranch, and he happens to be my best friend. We went to school together, and when he needed a job a few years ago, I got Dad to hire him on. With him around, I don't feel so lonely. Although he and his girlfriend are looking to get married, so I figure that will change pretty fast." Haven looked around the restaurant. "Do you feel like everyone's staring at us?"

Phillip glanced at the other diners before returning his attention to Haven. "No one's giving us a second thought. Don't worry, it's not like we're holding hands or anything. We're just friends having dinner."

Haven looked back at him. "I know. This is just so different."

Phillip lowered his voice. "Haven't you ever been on a date before?" Haven shook his head. "Not even with a girl?" Another shake of his head.

"I went out a few times, sort of a double date with friends, but I was pretty shy in school, and I think I've sort of figured out why."

"Yeah, you probably have. I, on the other hand, came bursting out of the closet when I was seventeen." Phillip grinned, and he saw Haven smile back at him. *Damn, the man was handsome, particularly when he smiled*, and Phillip felt a tingle of attraction. If they weren't in a crowded restaurant in rural Wyoming, he might....

"So what do you do for fun?" Haven's question pulled him back to reality, and he was saved from giving an immediate answer by Frankie returning with their meals, setting the plates in front of them.

"You be sure to let me know if anything isn't right," Frankie said with a smile before leaving the table, returning a few minutes later to fill their water glasses.

"So, you were saying," Haven prodded, as he cut a bite from his steak.

"Fun... right...." Phillip slipped the first bite of his beef into his mouth, the meat practically melting on his tongue. "I like to cook. I'm not much of an outdoor person, but when I was here last time, Dakota and Wally taught me how to ride, or at least the basics."

"So what else do you do in the city?" Haven asked softly.

"Go to clubs, hang out with friends, stuff like that," Phillip answered, and he could almost see a cloud move over Haven's face. "What is it?"

"We don't have anything like that here. All we got is the roller rink outside town and the VFW hall where they have dancing on Saturday night." Haven moved closer. "And there ain't no way I could ever go there with you."

"You don't have to compete, Haven. There aren't horses in the city, and there aren't places to ride ATVs, either."

"You mean you might like to go riding with me sometime?" Haven asked so sweetly, for a second Phillip almost thought he was back in high school. Then he remembered Haven's inexperience and thought it was possible that Haven could be asking from a social perspective.

"Of course, as long as you don't expect me to jump over any fences, ride fast, or turn corners." Phillip grinned and saw Haven laugh, eyes shining.

"Hey, what's this?" Haven's smile shriveled, and Phillip swallowed as he looked at the two men standing near their table. Phillip thought he recognized them from his last visit. He certainly recognized the face of the man nearest to him, especially the crooked nose courtesy of Wally. "Haven, who's your friend?" Jesus, these guys were something else.

"This is Phillip. He's from out of town," Haven said as he stood up, staring at both the men, making no effort to make introductions. "I suggest you go back to your table." The men looked at each other, obviously sharing one brain between them, before leaving, and Haven lowered himself into his chair. "I went to school with them too. They were on the football team with Kade."

"Let me guess, one too many blows to the head?" Phillip raised his eyebrows, and Haven smiled again. "There are guys like them everywhere."

"I suppose," Haven responded, but Phillip could tell that some of the fun was gone for Haven.

"Why don't we finish eating and we can leave," Phillip offered, and Haven nodded. They ate the rest of their meals in near silence. Phillip saw Haven continually scan the room nervously between bites. Phillip ate quickly, calling for the check, and blessedly soon they were outside, walking toward the truck. "Is there a place we can go to watch the stars?"

"I guess so," Haven said, sounding a little leery for a second. "You want to follow me?"

"Sure." Phillip climbed in the truck and waited for Haven's truck to pass before falling in behind. Turning out of the restaurant, Phillip kept his eyes on the taillights with the ram design as they wound their way out of town and into the nearly complete darkness of the countryside. Phillip followed close, knowing if he lost sight of Haven, he'd never find his way back. The truck began to climb, and then Phillip saw brake lights before Haven turned off the road, parking his truck in a clearing on top of what appeared to be a small rise.

"Is this okay?" Haven asked just before slamming the truck door closed.

Phillip got out and looked around, the truck light clicking off, casting them in darkness. A few lights could be seen in the distance, but mostly they were surrounded by blackness and millions of stars reaching from the sky overhead seemingly all the way to the ground in every direction. "It's perfect." Phillip heard a thunk and realized Haven had lowered the tailgate on his truck. Phillip joined him, using the tailgate as a bench, looking upward. "When I was a kid, my folks had a small piece of property on a river, and we used to go up for weekends. It was really quiet, and at night, you could see every star, just like this." Phillip pointed toward the heavenly map above, crickets chirping in the grass nearby. "There's the big dipper, and just over there in what looks like a 'W' is Cassiopeia. Orion's right there." Phillip moved his hand before shivering slightly as he leaned back against the cool metal.

The truck shifted, and Phillip heard Haven's footsteps. The truck door opened, and Phillip closed his eyes against the light. Hearing the door close, he opened them again as Haven rejoined him on the tailgate, spreading a blanket over the top of them. "The temperature drops fast some nights," he explained before going quiet for a while. "Show me more."

At first Phillip wasn't sure what Haven meant, his mind drifting from the stars to Haven's warmth right next to him and the feel of the hand just brushing his leg. Clearing his mind, Phillip slipped a hand from under the blanket. "Right over there is Perseus and Andromeda, and over there is Pegasus, the winged horse." Phillip let his voice fall away. "It's been a long time," he said to himself, trying to remember the last time he'd done something like this, and he found he couldn't. "Do you see the band of close stars that crosses the sky? That's the Milky Way, the rest of our galaxy. We're on one arm out toward the edge, and that's what we can see of the rest of it." Phillip let his voice trail off, since Haven didn't ask for more or even say anything.

A hand moved along Phillip's side, then slid into his, fingers curling together. "What's it like to be gay?" Haven asked very softly, almost like he was a child and said something he knew was bad.

"It's not like anything. It's part of who we are," Phillip answered, still staring up at the stars, but no longer seeing them, his entire consciousness zeroing in on the feel of Haven's skin against his. "We don't choose to be gay, and your mom or dad didn't do anything to make you gay. It's just part of how we're made." Phillip turned his head to look at Haven and found the other man looking back.

"But what's it like in the city? Are there guys everywhere?"

Phillip sighed. "Being gay and living in the city sounds like it would be a man buffet, but it's not. It's sort of the same as it is here. There are places like Dakota's where it's safe and you can be yourself, mostly bars and clubs. And there are places where you have to watch yourself, like at the restaurant tonight. And sometimes"—Phillip squeezed Haven's hand—"you find surprises in the most unlikely of places."

"Have you been with lots of guys?" Haven's voice drifted to his ears, and Phillip sighed.

"I guess you could say that, yes." Phillip wasn't too sure what he wanted to say on this topic but thought honesty was best.

"Have you been with anyone I know?"

Phillip rolled his head, looking up at the stars. "Yes. But that was a long time ago and how Dakota and I got to be friends." Phillip waited for another question, but none came. "Dakota and I met on a cruise, almost two years ago now I guess it would be. We had a nice time together, but after we returned home, Dakota and I talked on the phone and our relationship changed. We became friends. Then last summer when I visited, Wally came with me and kind of never left." Phillip felt himself smile. "That reminds me." Phillip chuckled softly.

"What's so funny?"

"That guy from the restaurant, the one with the crooked nose." Phillip couldn't stop his continued snickers.

"Yeah, Herbie, what about him?" Haven asked curiously. "He's one guy you don't want to mess with."

"Do you know how he got that nose?" Phillip knew he was having too much fun with this.

"I heard it was in some kind of fight, but for once he and his friends stayed pretty tight-lipped." Phillip felt Haven shift and saw the bigger man sit up. "You know something, don't you?"

"Yeah, he got that nose courtesy of Wally." Phillip started to laugh. At the time, no one had been laughing, but time and distance had ways of changing things. "He and some of his friends decided they weren't happy about Dakota and Wally. They came at them outside the steakhouse, and Wally laid the guy out like nobody's business."

"Wally?" Now Haven was laughing. "Dakota's Wally? That guy looks like he couldn't hurt anybody." Haven's laughter increased. "How'd he do it?"

"Wally may be small, but he knows how to fight. I think he's a black belt in something, but I've never asked him." Phillip let the mirth fade from his voice. "He's never been aggressive as far as I know, but he'll defend himself."

Phillip heard Haven heave a deep sigh. "It's not right that anyone has to, but I guess that comes with the territory."

Phillip tightened his fingers, squeezing Haven's hand. "I wish I could tell you it didn't, but I'm willing to bet you can take care of yourself." Phillip turned toward Haven, a hand sliding along a stubbled cheek. Leaning closer, he touched their lips together, unsure of how Haven would react after what had happened earlier. Keeping the kiss gentle, Phillip lightly tasted Haven's lips. Most of the guys he'd kissed had soft, smooth lips, but Haven's were slightly chapped and rough, like the rest of him—built for a life outdoors. Deepening the kiss slowly, Phillip felt Haven respond and shifted closer, fingers sliding through Haven's hair. Nothing about this man was smooth or soft, everything from his arms to his hair had been hardened by work, and damn if it wasn't the sexiest feeling ever.

Haven's lips parted slightly, and Phillip moved still closer, working his arms around him, kissing hard. He nearly broke the kiss to smile when he heard a tiny moan deep in Haven's throat. Strong arms wound around Phillip's waist, tugging him close as they continued kissing, Phillip losing himself in the moment.

Haven suddenly stilled. "What's wrong?" Phillip asked, and Haven shushed him.

"Listen. Something's wrong." Haven sat up, and Phillip could see his silhouette, still against the stars, head slightly cocked. Phillip didn't move, listening, but he wasn't sure what he was listening for. "Did you hear that?" Haven asked, and Phillip shook his head.

"No," Phillip whispered as he looked around, but everything looked the same. "What am I listening for?" Haven placed a finger over Phillip's mouth, and he resisted the urge to lick it.

"Did you hear that?" Haven asked very softly.

Phillip cocked his ear. He heard crickets and the occasional call of the cattle, but nothing else. "Is that it?"

"Yeah," Haven whispered. "I'm going to get a light." Haven slid off the tailgate, the truck shifting slightly with the change in weight.

"What is it?" Phillip asked following behind him.

"Sounds like a calf in trouble."

Phillip stopped moving and continued to listen. All he heard was a high-pitched sound from far away. Damn, Haven had good ears. The truck door opened, and Phillip watched Haven fumbling behind the seat, pulling out a flashlight, handing it to him before grabbing another. "Whose cattle are these, anyway?"

"Ours," Haven answered. "Those lights over there are my house"—Haven pointed—"and those are Dakota's. This is the very back of our land. If you want to stay here, that's fine."

"No." Phillip walked to the front of Haven's truck. "I'm coming with you."

"Then turn on your flashlight and walk slowly and carefully. The ground is uneven and there's probably barbed wire between us and the calf. Although I'm wondering how it could have gotten way out here. There shouldn't be any calves way out here."

Haven led the way down the rise, following what looked like a path through the grass and scrub. A glint of metal ahead was the only warning they had before they encountered the barbed wire fencing. Phillip could now hear what sounded almost like soft bleating as Haven bent, parting the wire. "Go on through, but be careful and don't go far. I'll be right behind you."

Phillip gingerly stepped through the wire, careful not to tear his pants, or his skin for that matter. On the other side, he stopped, holding the wire so Haven could get through. "I think it's over this way," Phillip said, gesturing with the light. He waited for Haven and followed him down the fence line, the bleating getting louder, and even to Phillip's unfamiliar ears, he could tell the animal was in pain.

"Over here," Haven called and rushed ahead. The calf had gotten itself caught in a piece of loose fencing, the barbed wire caught around its hind legs, and it kept struggling to get away. "Shhh," Haven began to croon lightly. "It's okay, little guy. We're here to help you."

Phillip shone his light on the calf's legs. They were red with blood. He had no idea how badly it was hurt, but even with Haven soothing it, the calf kept struggling, making the injury worse. "Can you get him free?" Phillip asked, having no idea what to do.

"I don't think so, not without hurting him worse. I need to call my dad." Haven pulled out his phone and hesitated. "You need to get back to your truck, because if my dad finds you here, he'll flip." Phillip pulled out his phone, dialing in the light of the phone keypad. "Who are you calling?"

"Wally. He'll know what to do, and he'll be able to help him." Phillip pressed the green button, watching as Haven held the calf down, still crooning to it. The phone was answered. "Wally, we need you. Haven and I are at the back on their land, and one of his calves is caught in some wire. It's bleeding."

"Phillip," he heard Dakota's voice say. "Slow down and tell me where you are."

"I'm not sure." Phillip huffed softly. "Haven and I went to a small rise, and we were looking at the stars when we heard a calf in trouble." Phillip knew he was talking really fast, but his heart pounded with excitement that only increased whenever he heard the pained bleating of the calf.

"Ask Haven where you are. Wally and I are on the way."

"Haven, where are we?" Phillip asked, turning toward where Haven was half hugging the calf to keep him still.

"Tell him we're at the back of our property near Hump Hill. He should know where that is." Haven looked up at him, obviously extremely concerned.

"Did you hear that?" Phillip asked.

"Yes. I know where it is. We'll be there in a few minutes." Phillip heard an engine start as Dakota hung up the phone.

"They're on their way," Phillip told Haven, slowly stepping closer to the calf. "Is there anything I can do?"

"Hold his head and shoulders. I'm going to try to still his legs so he can't hurt himself worse," Haven said, and Phillip knelt on the ground, moisture seeping into his clothes. "Hold him like this. Use your weight." Haven kept his voice level, and Phillip felt some of his own excitement fade away. "He's not very old, so you should be able to hold him down, and talk to him, low and calm. He'll react to your excitement, so remain as calm as possible."

Phillip did as Haven asked, the small calf pushing back against him, and he used all his weight to keep him still, talking softly. "It's okay, boy. We're here to help and won't hurt you." Phillip felt the pressure from the calf lessen as he rested on the ground. "Don't move. It's okay," Phillip said, and the warm calf looked back at him with huge dark eyes that shone in the flashlights.

Phillip heard a vehicle approaching and then the night quieted again. "Phillip, Haven!" Dakota called.

"We're down here," Haven answered. "Be careful of the barbed wire."

Footsteps got closer, with the muffled voices becoming more and more distinct. Then Wally knelt next to him, looking the calf over. "Kota, would you give me a pair of clippers? I need to cut away this wire." Flashlights moved around, and Phillip continued to hold the calf, whispering softly into his ear. "Guys, I'm going to sedate him. His legs are pretty torn up, but I can't see much out here."

Phillip saw Wally prepare a needle in the light of a flashlight before injecting the calf. Beneath his body, he felt the calf go limp, and he waited a few seconds before standing up. "Is he going to be okay?" Phillip asked Wally softly.

"I'm going to do everything I can, but right now I can't see well enough to do anything." Wally turned to Haven. "Can you carry him?"

"Yes," Haven answered.

"Let me go ahead," Dakota said, and he walked toward the fence, clipping the wire to make a path. Haven cradled the sleeping calf in his arms, and Phillip held the light for him, illuminating the ground ahead of them until they reached Dakota's truck.

"Put him in back. The bed's lined, so he won't get hurt. We need to get him back to the ranch as quickly as possible. The sedative should only last an hour or so. I didn't want to give him too much," Wally said as he climbed in the driver's seat. "I'll meet you there," Wally said, closing the door and lowering the window.

"Wally, wait," Phillip called, and he climbed into the back of the truck, sitting next to the calf. "I'll ride with him."

"Okay, Phillip, but it's going to be bumpy," Wally warned, and Phillip handed his keys to Haven.

"Give these to Dakota. I'll see you at the ranch," Phillip said, and Haven nodded. Before Wally put the truck in gear, Phillip leaned over the edge and gave Haven a quick kiss before settling back into the bed of the truck. Phillip felt the truck slip into gear, and he steadied the calf as they backed away and took off down the dark road as fast as Wally dared. Phillip paid no attention to where they were going. He simply stroked the calf's neck and made sure it didn't get too jostled.

Finally, after a whirlwind of speed, they pulled into the drive and up to the barn. "Mario!" Wally yelled as he climbed out of the truck, slamming the door.

"Yeah," Mario answered, hurrying over, the screen door to his cabin banging behind him.

"Could you carry this calf into the surgery?" Wally asked, and Mario lowered the tailgate. "Be careful of his legs. He tore them up pretty bad."

Mario gingerly lifted the calf out of the truck and carried him into the barn, with Wally right behind. Phillip had no idea what to do. He wanted to follow Wally and see if he could help, but he figured he'd be in the way, so he stayed outside, waiting for Haven and Dakota. Both of their vehicles arrived a few minutes later.

Getting out of the trucks, they looked at Phillip, who told them where the calf was. "You want a beer?" Dakota asked Haven, and he nodded, while Phillip stared openmouthed at both of them.

"That little calf is in there hurt, and you're going to have a beer?" Phillip marched over to both of them, ready to kick some ass.

"Phillip," Dakota said calmly, "there's nothing we can do but stay out of Wally's way. I know this is upsetting for you, but this happens sometimes. We try to help, but mostly you have to let nature do her thing." Phillip felt Dakota's hand on his shoulder, and he almost shrugged it off. "You got a look into those big calf eyes, didn't you?"

"Yeah, so?" Phillip asked indignantly.

"Go on inside." Dakota tilted his head toward the door. "I'll be right in after I check on Wally." Dakota walked toward the barn. Phillip led Haven inside, the two men sitting on the sofa.

"You did great, Phillip," Haven said as he bumped their shoulders. "Although it wasn't exactly how I had the evening pictured, you know?"

"I know, but if we hadn't been there?" Phillip looked over at Haven, and the look on his face told him all he needed to know. "Do you want to wait? I can call you when I hear from Wally."

"Thanks, that'd be great." Haven leaned close, and Phillip met him halfway, the two men sharing a gentle kiss. "I'm going to have enough to explain to my dad." Haven looked toward the barn through the window. "I know the calf's in good hands." He walked toward the door. "I'll probably see you tomorrow, and if the weather's nice, maybe we can go for that ride."

"I'd like that," Phillip answered, watching Haven leave. Phillip saw him wave to Dakota and then get in his truck, taillights shining as he turned out of the drive. A few seconds later, the door banged closed as Dakota walked across the floor to the kitchen, returning with a couple beers.

"One of the things you learn in this business is not to get attached to the livestock." Dakota flopped on the sofa, slipping off his boots before reclining with his stocking feet on the coffee table, handing Phillip a beer. "I had to be about ten when my dad gave me a calf to raise. I fed him, petted him, talked to him, and basically fell in love with him. I even took him to the fair and won a ribbon. I was so proud, and so was Dad." Dakota sipped from the bottle before getting up, returning with a framed picture from the mantle. "That's me and Clyde at the fair. What isn't in the picture is the look on my face when Dad told me that Clyde was going to be auctioned off. I called my dad every name in the book, and he let me because he knew I needed to learn that the livestock weren't pets, but our business." Dakota took another swig of his beer.

"What'd you do?" Phillip asked, gulping the beer. After the last hour or so he needed it.

"I cried for a while, that is until Dad handed me the check from the auction and told me it was mine."

Phillip looked over at Dakota before smacking the man on the arm. "You bastard," Phillip cried through his laughter. "You really had me going there."

"It's true, Phillip. Don't get me wrong, I hope the calf is going to be okay, but we can't get emotional over it. Haven knows that too. If we did, we'd go crazy when we had to take the steers to market." Dakota finished his beer, setting the bottle on the table.

"It's just hard."

"I know, but it's something you learn pretty quick around here. That is, unless you're Wally."

The door opened and Wally walked in, looking tired. "He's going to be fine. I have him lightly sedated so he'll sleep, and after a few days he'll be up and about." Wally yawned and Dakota got up, throwing away his bottle before taking Wally by the hand, leading him down the hallway to bed.

Fishing his phone out of his pocket, Phillip dialed. "It's Phillip," he said, when Haven answered. "That calf is going to be fine."

"Thanks for calling." Haven became quiet, and Phillip heard him moving around. "I had a nice time tonight. Thank you for dinner and for helping."

"You're welcome. I'll see you tomorrow for our ride." Phillip smiled as he hung up the phone. Finishing his beer, he tossed out the bottle before turning out the lights and heading to bed, thinking of Haven.

## Chapter Five

*GOD, what a night.* Haven forced his eyes open, dawn just beginning to brighten the windows. Phillip—the name popped into his head, and he smiled when he remembered the look of indignation on the man's face at Dakota's remark. You had to like a man who'd hold an injured calf and ride in the back of a truck with him just to make sure he didn't get jostled too much. Staring at the ceiling, he remembered other things from last night as well: the touch of Phillip's lips on his, the excitement that coursed through his veins like crystal fire when Phillip's body pressed to his. Haven closed his eyes, fingers sliding down his chest and belly, curling around his shaft. After years of being alone, Haven had developed a vivid imagination, and it went into overdrive as pictures of Phillip flashed in his mind. Phillip standing at the foot of his bed, his shirt sliding off his shoulders, tanned skin disappearing into the waistband of designer jeans. A smile ghosted over Haven's face as he reached to the imaginary Phillip, the buttons easily popping undone, fabric falling away, Phillip standing hard and ready in front of him.

"Haven, you up yet!" Like the proverbial needle scratching a record, the voice shattered his fantasy, and Haven sighed as he released himself, throwing back the covers.

"Yeah, I'm up, for God's sake," Haven called through the door, yawning widely.

"That's enough of that, boy," Haven heard from outside his door.

Ignoring his dad, Haven yawned again before pulling on some clothes and heading to the bathroom. He had no idea how he was going to make it through the day, as tired as he was, but he'd done it before, and he'd do it again. The animals needed care, and there was work to be done, and it wouldn't do itself. Haven heard movement in the house as he crossed the hall and closed the bathroom door behind him, blinking when he turned on the lights. Running cool water, he splashed some onto his face before reaching for the shaving cream, smearing it on his face. As he finished, Haven finally started to wake up.

Walking into the kitchen, dressed and ready, Haven saw his dad sitting at the table, watching the farm report on TV. "You know, you could have made breakfast for once," Haven groused as his dad sipped coffee.

"No sassing me, boy." The television shut off, and Haven's dad got up, setting his mug in the sink. Haven poured himself a bowl of cereal, glaring at his father as he ate. "You got something to say?"

Haven contemplated voicing his frustrations, but he held his tongue. Not that he knew why, but it just didn't seem right. Returning his attention to his breakfast, Haven grumbled softly as he finished eating and left the kitchen, heading outside to work. "Morning, Kade," Haven called when he saw his friend's truck pull up.

"Morning, Haven." The truck door slammed shut. "What's on for today?" Kade walked over to where Haven stood, yawning into the sun. "You look like hell. What happened? Did you stay out with a girl?"

Haven ignored the connotation. "I was up late because one of the calves got into the north range, and we found it tangled in some barbed wire."

"What were you doing out there? Unless...." Kade grinned slyly. "You were out at Hump Hill with some girl, you dog."

"Kade," he said, rolling his eyes, trying to get him back on track.

"So who was it?" He obviously wasn't going to let this go.

"I wasn't out there with a girl, okay?" Haven said softly, cutting off Kade before he could continue. "The calf's hind legs got cut up pretty bad. We called Wally and Dakota. The calf's at their place, and I need to go get it before Dad has some sort of fit," Haven said between his teeth. This particular line of questioning wasn't making him comfortable.

Kade's eyes narrowed, and he looked toward the barn and then back at the house before pulling Haven into the barn. "Do you have something you want to tell me?"

"Like what?" He played dumb, hoping this would go away. The last thing he wanted was to be having this discussion, and he could feel his heart pounding in his chest, vision swimming around the edges.

"Haven," Kade coaxed, "I don't care. You're my best friend, have been for years, and that's not going to change." Kade stared at him piercingly, waiting. "Come on, you were out at Hump Hill with that friend of Dakota's. And I bet you weren't there to look at the stars," Kade added sarcastically.

"Well, that's kind of why Phillip and I went there," Haven said very softly.

"So you are gay?" Kade asked in a whisper. "I knew it."

"How?" Haven asked, swallowing hard. *Did everyone know?*

"You never dated, and you always got nervous and shy around Penny and her friends. At first I thought you were scared around girls...." Kade stopped, his mouth breaking into a smile. "It's cool, Haven. I won't tell anyone. Does your dad know?"

"Good God, no." Haven nearly had a seizure at the thought of how his father would react. The man had never been the best dad, let alone a paragon of understanding and fatherly support. "I figure I'll tell him in ten or twenty years when he's too old to take a swing at me."

"Do you want me to go pick up the calf?"

"No, I'll do it this afternoon sometime. We need to get our work done here, and Dad isn't likely to miss it right away. Besides, we need to take a look at the fences over there—that calf got into the range somehow."

"Okay, I'll saddle up and take a look once I'm finished in the barn." Kade moved away, already getting to work, and Haven called Jake in from his paddock. He could hardly believe Kade's reaction, and Haven smiled to himself as he felt his stomach unclench and his heart rate return to normal. He'd honestly thought he'd lose his friends if they found out. And while he wasn't going to be shouting from the rooftops, it was nice to know some people would accept him. Leading Jake into his stall, Haven started the saddling process, pushing other thoughts away for now. There were herds to check on, and Lord knew, plenty of maintenance chores to get done. It was going to be a busy day, and he needed to get started if he wanted to go riding with Phillip later.

LATE in the afternoon, exhausted from working double-time, Haven slipped off Jake, leading him into his stall. The horse immediately went for his water before munching from the hay in the manger. Patting the horse's neck, Haven murmured, "I'll let you rest for a while." After another soft pat, Haven left the stall, closing the door behind him.

Walking to the house, he noticed his father's truck was gone. With a sigh of relief, Haven strode toward the door, pulling it open and walking through the house, the screen door banging behind him. Opening the refrigerator, he nearly reached for a beer, but went for a Coke instead, popping it open and gulping it down. Throwing the can in the trash, he reached for another before closing the door.

"Haven," Kade said from outside just before opening the door. "I found a small break in the fence to the north range," Kade told him as he walked over, shirt sweated through, and Haven handed him a Coke as well. "I repaired it, but...." Kade looked at him strangely. "The fence almost looked cut. I know it sounds crazy, but I don't think I'm wrong."

"Who would want to cut our fences?" Haven asked out loud, but he didn't really expect an answer.

"If you were asking your dad, he'd say the Holdens, but that's stupid. You said yourself that Dakota and Wally hurried over to help last night. Why would they do that if they'd cut the fence. I mean, the feud with your dad and Mr. Holden has gone on for years and is the stuff of lore around town, but Jefferson Holden's been confined to bed for years."

"Maybe someone's stirring up trouble," Haven proposed, half thinking out loud. "Did you fix the break?"

"Yeah. Did it right too. I also walked the rest of the line, and it's solid as anything." Kade finished his soda, throwing the can away. "What? You look like you're figuring out a solution to world peace."

Haven shook his head. "It's nothing. But I think we need to check all our fences just in case. If someone is causing trouble, we need to make sure we know."

"Let me cool off and I'll start," Kade said.

Haven looked at the clock. "It's near quitting time for today. That can wait till tomorrow. I'm gonna head over and pick up the calf."

"I noticed Jake's still saddled, you want me to put him out?"

"No." Haven checked out the windows. "I'm going riding with Phillip."

Kade smiled. "Good for you. I'll cover with your dad if you aren't back." He grabbed another Coke and headed back outside while Haven checked the mail, throwing it on the table as his phone rang.

"Haven, it's Phillip. Are we still on for a ride?" he asked excitedly.

"I'm just about to leave, so I'll see you in a few minutes." Haven said goodbye and hung up, sliding his phone back into his pocket. Walking across the yard, he checked everything as he did, making sure nothing was out of place before leading Jake out of his stall.

The ride to the Holden ranch didn't take long, since he could use trails that were more direct than the road, emerging from the scrub near one of Dakota's ranges and following the fence to the house. Things seemed quiet, and Haven dismounted, looking around as a troop of dogs walked up to him, sniffing his legs before sitting down, looking up at him expectantly.

"Phillip will be right out," Wally said as he emerged from the barn, the dogs rushing over to him, jumping over each other in their excitement for attention. "Why don't you hitch him to the post, and you can see your calf. He's doing fine." Haven complied and followed Wally through the barn to the door out back. "He's walking a little stiffly, but his muscles weren't too badly injured, so he should heal up quick. Just keep him segregated from the rest of the herd for a few days."

"Thanks, Wally," Haven said, shaking the man's hand.

"Hey, you two!" Haven heard Dakota call from behind him.

"Hey, Dakota," Haven called, waiting as the other two men shared a brief kiss. "Kade checked the fence and found what looked like cut wire."

Both Dakota and Wally stared back at him. "Why would anyone do that?" Wally asked, shaking his head.

"I think someone may be stirring up trouble. If my dad had found the break, he'd blame you loudly and to anyone who'd listen. So tomorrow, Kade and I are going to check the remainder of our fences."

"We'll do the same," Dakota said with a nod as Phillip walked toward them. "You two have a good ride, and when you get back, we'll help you get the calf home."

"Thanks," Haven said before turning and walking toward Phillip.

"I saddled Sophie for you, Phillip. She's in the first stall," Wally called, and Phillip thanked him before he opened the stall door, leading the horse out into the yard. Haven held the reins while Phillip mounted the horse. Untying Jake from the post, Haven easily swung onto his back.

"There's a trail that leads from behind the house, along the range, and out toward the river," Dakota instructed as he approached from the barn. "Stay away from Schian. He'll roar at the horses. And have a good ride."

"Thanks for the warning," Haven said with a smile, and he took the lead, easily finding the trail.

"You didn't get in trouble with your dad, did you?" Phillip asked from behind him.

"No. He was asleep by the time I got home. The trouble will come when I bring home the calf and he asks how it got injured, but I figure I'll make up something plain. It happens sometimes, so hopefully he won't think too much about it." Haven slowed Jake to a walk. "I've never been here before," Haven said as he looked around. "I thought our place was nice, but this has it beat."

Phillip pointed toward a stand of trees. "That's where Wally's lion is. I saw it yesterday—he's really something."

"I can't believe he keeps a lion," Haven commented as Jake walked leisurely, swaying beneath him. Jake tensed beneath him as a roar ripped over the range.

"You should try being woken up at five in the morning to a lion's roar. This morning I thought I was on the Serengeti instead of in Wyoming." Phillip laughed and Haven found himself smiling. "Wally took me along when he fed him. Schian moved away when Wally opened the gate and put in the food. Once Wally moved away, Schian ate and then rolled over so Wally could pet his tummy."

"You're kidding." Haven shook his head—that was just too much.

"It gets better. As he rubbed his belly, the big baby began to purr whenever he exhaled. You could hear it twenty feet away." Phillip chuckled and Haven thought that was something he had to see sometime.

They rode through the range, along the path toward the river, conversation trickling away. Haven loved this view: the range, the trees by the river, the Tetons in the background. His saddle creaking as they moved, Haven loved being on horseback, and with Phillip right behind him, he could practically feel the other man's gaze. As they approached the water and the shade, the temperature dropped, and Haven slipped off his hat, wiping his brow. "We can take a rest here if you like," Haven said, slipping off the horse and letting him munch on the grass.

Phillip struggled but managed a less-than-graceful trip to the ground, which Haven did his best not to notice. The water skipped over rocks, the level already going down, the rain from a few days ago simply a memory. "Dakota told me once that he used to go swimming here," Phillip commented as he bent near the water, dipping in his hand. "It's a bit cold."

Haven watched Phillip straighten up before walking to him, standing close enough to feel his heat. "Do you want to swim, or—"

Arms wound around his neck and Phillip kissed him. With everything that had happened, Haven almost thought he'd imagined those kisses under the stars, but now every detail flooded back. This time he wasn't going to be a bystander, and he tugged Phillip close, deepening the kiss. Those lips on his felt like heaven, and damn, if this was what kissing was like, he should have tried it years ago.

"Haven," Phillip said, pulling his lips away, "what about the horses?"

He looked around, both animals were happily munching. "They'll be fine for a few minutes." That was all he needed to say, because Phillip captured his lips again, kissing hard. Haven jumped slightly as a pair of hands rested on his butt, fingers squeezing slightly. For a second, his mind protested, but Phillip's lips kissed away anything other than the feel and taste of those lips on his. Eventually Haven had to come up for air and broke the kiss, breathing like he'd just run a race.

"You're a great kisser, you know that?" Phillip said with a grin.

Haven widened his eyes. "No."

"No one's ever told you that?" Phillip moved closer again.

"I've never kissed anyone before except my aunts, and they don't count." Haven looked at the ground, shuffling his feet.

"You've never...." Phillip stopped moving, and Haven thought he was going to leave or something. "You've never done anything, have you?" Haven shook his head, his humiliation complete. It wasn't that he hadn't wanted to, but he lived in rural Wyoming, and it wasn't as though he'd had lots of opportunities. "It's okay, Haven." He felt a finger slip under his chin. "There's certainly nothing to be ashamed of."

He lifted his eyes and saw the grin on Phillip's face. "You don't think I'm some kind of freak?"

"No." Phillip shook his head slowly, inching closer, kissing him again. "Not at all." The breeze rustled through the trees, and Haven let go of his worries, allowing himself to get lost in the kiss. This time, he let his hands wander, skimming them over Phillip's back.

"We should probably continue our ride," Haven commented lightly, not really wanting to let go of Phillip, but he could hear the horses moving around behind him.

"I suppose," Phillip said softly.

"Did you ever go camping as a kid?" Haven asked, and Phillip shook his head. "Sometimes my friends and I would camp out on the range. We'd make snacks and hike away from the house. We were never really very far away, but it felt like we were. I haven't slept out in a long time, and I thought it might be fun."

Phillip looked up at him, eyes wide. "Are you asking me to camp out with you?"

"Yeah. I know it's lame. Forget it." Haven stepped back, taking Jake's reins.

"I'd love to, Haven." Phillip touched his cheek very softly. "Just tell me when." Phillip kissed him again before climbing back on his horse. Haven mounted as well, and they headed back toward the house, and Haven felt himself grinning the entire way.

In the yard, Phillip dismounted and led Sophie into the barn. Wally came out, followed by the pack of dogs. "If you'd like, I can drive the calf back to your place."

"That'd be great," Haven said, and he waited for Phillip to come back out.

"Then we'll meet you there in a while."

Haven leaned down, and Phillip stood on his tiptoes so they could share a quick kiss.

"Go on, lover boy, Phillip and I will see you soon."

Haven waved and walked his horse toward home. Riding up to the barn, he saw that his dad's truck was still gone, and he relaxed somewhat. At least he'd have a little less explaining to do. Slipping off Jake, he led him to his stall. After taking off his saddle, he left him to eat and drink, waiting in the waning evening light for Wally.

Hearing the sound of tires on the gravel drive, Haven put Jake's saddle away before giving the horse a carrot and walking outside. Wally's truck, with a small trailer on behind it, pulled to a stop near the barn. "Thank you," Haven said and walked around the back to help unload the calf.

"It's no problem. I'm happy I could help." Phillip joined them, and Haven shared a smile with him before opening the trailer door. The calf immediately moved toward them, and Haven used the rope Wally had around the calf's neck to guide him into an empty paddock. "He should stay where you can keep an eye on him for a few days, and then you can go ahead and put him with the rest of the herd," Wally said.

"I will," Haven agreed as the three of them leaned on the paddock fence, watching the calf explore his temporary space. The sound of tires from behind him made Haven tense, and he turned around to see his father's truck coming down the drive.

"What's going on, Haven?" his father asked, the questions starting almost as soon as his dad's feet hit the ground. "Who are these people, and what are they doing here?" Haven saw his dad looking over everything. "What is that calf doing in the paddock?"

Haven felt his stomach twist, and it took him a second to find his voice. Why his dad made him act that way, he had no idea. "I found him injured last night, and Wally took care of him. He and Phillip were just bringing him back." As if to demonstrate, the calf ran over to where they were standing, his injured legs plain to see. "He got caught in some wire."

"Mr. Jessup." Wally stepped forward, and Haven had to admire how calm he seemed, whereas Haven felt like a wreck, wondering how his father was going to react. "Haven called us in time, and the calf has minimal muscle damage. He should be fine in a few days. I left Haven instructions," Wally said as he walked toward his truck before turning to Haven. "If he has any problems, give me a call."

Haven walked to both men, shaking first Wally's and then Phillip's hand, holding the latter's a little longer than necessary. Wanting to say something, but knowing he didn't dare, he hoped the look in his eyes said enough.

"How much do I owe you?" Haven's dad asked, approaching Wally.

"Nothing at all," Wally answered with a smile. "Just being neighborly." Opening his door, Wally climbed in the truck while Phillip walked around the back, closing the door on the trailer before getting into the truck. The engine started, and Haven watched his friends drive away, an ache in his heart. Being near Phillip had been wonderful, and Haven had to stop himself from whirling around to glare at his father. Wally and Phillip had been more than nice as well as helpful, and the way his dad had treated his friends was downright rude.

"Boy, you've got some explaining to do." His father's voice boomed from behind him. "I come home from town and find a couple of faggots from next door on my ranch, bringing back one of my calves, and no one"—Haven felt himself cringe under his father's intense gaze—"bothered to tell me what was going on." His dad's look softened a little, but his voice remained just as intense. "You are to have no contact with anyone from the Holden ranch, least of all that faggot vet and his friend—"

"Dad, for God's sake, you think he's going to make the calf gay? They helped us out and didn't even charge you anything." Haven could feel his own temper beginning to simmer. "If they hadn't, we'd have lost the calf. Instead, he's safe, whole, and in our paddock. What's the problem?" Haven felt his voice get louder. "Are you jealous? Is that it? Are you jealous because their ranch is more prosperous than ours? It's sure as hell a lot bigger and definitely nicer. Lord knows it's not as run-down."

His father stepped closer, standing toe to toe, and Haven half expected the older man to take a swing at him. "If things aren't up to your standards," his father said, sarcasm plain in his voice, "then you need to work harder around here."

"Work harder!" Haven's temper flared. "You don't do a goddamn thing around here except sit in your office all day. There aren't enough men, and you haven't replaced any of the equipment in years." Haven exploded, saying, "Everything is on its last leg, held together with baling twine and barbed wire. If you're jealous of what Mr. Holden has, then it's your own fault."

"Boy"—his father seethed between clenched teeth—"if you're not happy here, you can always find a place you like better."

"And leave you to handle everything around here?" Haven swept his hands around the yard. "The place would completely fall apart, and if I remember right, Grandpa left me part of the ranch."

"In trust," his father added, eyes blazing.

"Until I turned twenty-one, which I am now," Haven said, boldly challenging his father even as his insides quivered at his rebellion.

"Haven!" his father snapped, "you watch yourself. You're still my son, and you'll show me the proper respect."

"Respect is earned, Dad," Haven retorted, leaving the implication of what he meant unsaid. The older man glared at him, and Haven braced himself to be hit, but nothing came, and eventually his father stepped back, his expression remaining as hard as ever.

"I meant what I said, Haven. You stay away from the Holdens and anyone else on that ranch. I will not have it! If I see you anywhere near any of them, so help me, I'll kick you off this ranch and out of town so fast it'll make your head spin." Haven watched as his dad spun around, striding back toward the house before wheeling around again. "Just so we're clear," his father said, pointing at him, "I will not have any son of mine hanging around with fags for any reason. Do I make myself plain?"

Haven didn't answer. He couldn't. To do so would betray people he thought of as friends, and he couldn't outright lie to his dad, so he said nothing, knowing his father would take the lack of an argument as acceptance. Refusing to watch his dad anymore, Haven turned and hurried into the barn, kicking the bucket near the door down the aisle, the metal rattling and banging as it bounced on the concrete. It didn't make him feel any better, not one bit. Just when he was beginning to understand his own feelings about who he was, his father's bigotry and irrational hatred reared its ugly head… again. In school, he'd wanted to play basketball. He loved the game, but his dad had flatly refused— "Too many blacks." Only his father hadn't been quite so politically correct. "Play football, it'll make a man out of you like it did me."

*Well, Dad,* Haven sighed as he thought, *it didn't do much for me, and look at the man it made out of you.* Picking up the bucket, he tried to push out the sizable dent before setting it back out of the way.

"You okay?" Kade said from the doorway.

"Yeah." Haven looked toward the house. "Just… ahhh!" He desperately wanted to take a swing at something, but knew that wouldn't do any good.

"I know, I kind of heard," Kade said sheepishly. "What are you going to do? I mean, you like Phillip, right?"

"Yeah," Haven answered. He really did, and it pissed him off no end that his dad thought he could dictate who his son spent his time with and who he could be friends with. "Screw him," Haven said, gesturing rudely toward the house before lowering his hands. "Why are you still here?"

"I decided to get the fences checked anyway," Kade answered with a smile. "I'll finish them tomorrow. I found a few weak spots as well, but we'll need fresh wire to fix them properly."

"We can do that tomorrow," Haven told him. "Now, don't you have somewhere else to be?" Haven did his best to smile. It wasn't Kade's fault his father was such an ass.

"Yeah, I'm taking Penny out tonight." Haven returned Kade's wave as his friend walked away, and he heard a truck pull out of the drive as his phone began to ring.

"This is Haven," he answered without looking at the display.

"It's Phillip. Is everything okay? From what you'd said, I was concerned when your dad showed up. Did he yell at you once we left?" Phillip's voice had an edge to it.

"Yeah, he was his usual sparkling self," Haven answered sarcastically, and he heard Phillip growl through the phone. "What?" Haven figured after meeting his dad, Phillip would run for the hills; most of his friends had. And he braced himself for Phillip's response.

"That man needs to be taught simple manners. I'm sorry, because I know he's your dad, but that man is a complete ass! Wally helped him out, and he treated him and you like dirt." Phillip sounded angry, and Haven swallowed, realizing Phillip was standing up for him in his own way. "I was hoping he'd pull something so Wally could clean his clock."

"Phillip," Haven looked around making sure "the ass"—he snickered when he thought of it—wasn't around. "It wouldn't do any good. I don't know why, but anything to do with Dakota and his dad sends him over the edge. I used to think he was jealous, and then I thought it was because Dakota's gay, but that's not it, although he's about as accepting in that area as you'd expect." Haven cringed at the thought of his father finding out he was gay. The way he'd spat out the names he'd called Dakota, Haven could only imagine how he'd react with him. Haven forced his mind back on track. "Whatever it is between them goes back a lot further than any of us."

The other end of the line became very quiet, and Haven thought for a second that Phillip had hung up. "Look, Haven, if seeing me is going to cause you all this trouble, I'll understand if you want to back away."

Haven held his breath, wondering if this was Phillip's way of backing out. Not that he could blame the guy—part of him screamed to crawl back in his shell for sheer self-preservation. But another part, a growing part, longed for the simple freedom of being who he was. "If that's what you want, Phillip."

More silence. "It's not. But I don't want to make things hard on you."

"You're not. He is," Haven said softly. "Do you still want to go camping sometime?" God, Haven knew he was probably taking his life into his hands, but damn it, his father could not be allowed to dictate his life. He liked Phillip, and the man awakened feelings Haven had never had before. Maybe he was young and stupid, or maybe it was just sheer bullheadedness, but he knew he wanted to see Phillip again, very much.

"Yeah, I would. But I don't want you getting in trouble."

"Phillip, I'm not a teenager or some kid. I'm a man. I can take whatever trouble he wants to dish out." Where that came from Haven wasn't sure, but it felt good to say it. "Why don't we plan on Friday night if the weather's good?"

"I'm looking forward to it," Phillip answered, his smile almost coming through the phone. Then his voice lowered, becoming deeper and more resonant. Haven felt it slip through his body, his jeans becoming just a little tighter, and he adjusted things for comfort. "It'll be fun. You and me alone together under the stars...." Phillip left the rest unsaid, and Haven swallowed hard to stop the small moan that threatened to escape.

"Haven, you coming in to eat?" His father's voice carried into the barn.

"I gotta go, but I'll definitely call you later." Haven heard Phillip say his quick goodbye and then disconnect. Dang, he could hardly wait till Friday.

## Chapter Six

EXCITEMENT rolled off Phillip as he worked with Wally getting the enclosure near Schian cleaned out. "What's going in here?" Phillip asked, as he pulled the weeds Wally had told him needed to be eradicated from the area.

"I have a Bengal tiger coming in from the same circus where I got Schian. They're going to be in the area in a few days, and they called and asked if I could take Kahn. They said his behavior is getting too erratic for them to handle in the shows anymore." Wally stood up, looking over at him.

"Let me guess, either you took him or they were going to put him down." Phillip didn't need confirmation from Wally; he knew the man too well. "So why are we pulling these weeds. Won't he just stomp the plants down anyway?"

"He will, but these are poisonous to the cattle, and I don't want them spreading. I also figured they might hurt the cats, so I'm killing two birds with one stone." Wally went back to work, pulling the weeds and tossing them into the barrow situated in the sun. "So what's going on with you and Haven? I haven't seen him in a few days. Are you guys okay?"

Phillip looked up from where he was working. "Everything's fine. We're going camping tonight. I'm not sure where, but I'm looking forward to it." He added the weeds to his pile and began looking for the next patch.

"You... going"—Wally grunted over some stubborn plants before landing on his butt in a spray of dirt—"camping?" Wally snickered as he threw the weeds onto the pile, grabbing another clump. "I never thought I'd see the day. Heck, I never thought I'd see you go a whole week without wearing designer jeans."

Phillip tossed a clump of weeds in Wally's direction, just missing him on purpose. "I bought several pairs of Wranglers just for this trip." Phillip stood up, trying to look around at his butt. "I don't think they do a damn thing for me."

Wally laughed outright. "Maybe not, but think how Haven looks in his." Wally tossed the clump back at him, and Phillip dodged, losing his footing, and now it was his turn to bounce on his ass.

"Funny," Phillip said, chuckling, as Wally collapsed in fits of laughter. "I was thinking…." Phillip's mirth died away. "We could build an exercise area for the cats." Wally stopped laughing, looking at Phillip quizzically, obviously intrigued. "As I see it, you can't take them out for walks, so what if we built a square exercise area?" Phillip got up and walked off an area near the enclosures. "Up to now, you've sort of connected the two areas for Schian, but you can't do that anymore." Phillip paced out his design. "So what if we build a big square or rectangle here and connect it with gates to each of the enclosures. That way one animal could use it at a time for exercise. You could then control who has the access."

Wally slapped him on the back excitedly. "I knew if I kept you around long enough, you'd be useful," Wally said, laughing. Phillip took off after the smaller man and stopped dead in his tracks as a menacing roar split the afternoon.

"That's not fair," Phillip groused as he slowly moved back to where he was working. "You've got the lion on your side."

"It's okay, Schian." Wally walked to the enclosure, talking softly to the imposing lion. "We were just playing." Phillip watched as the big cat rolled onto his back, paws in the air, expecting Wally to rub his belly, purring up a storm. "Can't right now, I've got work to do," Wally explained as he backed away, as though the animal could understand him.

Returning to work, they scanned the area for the menacing weeds, but found no more. "So I take it you like my idea."

"I really do," Wally added with a nod of his head. "We can start building it when you get back from your camping trip—that is, if you aren't dead on your feet from lack of sleep."

"You're serious?" Phillip didn't know if he should be pleased or upset at being volunteered. He settled on pleased. If he was going to stay, he needed to be useful. After all, this wasn't a dude ranch. He'd learned that on his last visit.

"Sure. I'll measure out the dimensions and go to town to get the supplies. It's not complicated. It just takes some effort, and the kitties will love it." Wally grabbed the wheelbarrow, carting the weeds to a pit nearby for dumping while Phillip gathered up the tools.

"What should I take camping?" Phillip asked as they walked back to the house.

"The essentials, a change of clothes, a couple of blankets, a pillow, condoms, lube...."

"I'm serious."

"Just pack what you need for overnight. I'm sure Haven will have most everything else." Wally set the wheelbarrow near the mulch pile outside the barn. "But I was serious about the condoms and lube. I get the feeling Haven hasn't had much experience, and you're going to need to help him. Be the loving mentor we all wish we'd had when we were coming out."

Phillip stopped in his tracks, gaping. "I don't want to be his mentor, and I don't want this to be something that's... God, I don't know what I want, but I know what I don't."

Wally walked over to him. "You don't want it to be like it was with Dakota or Mario. You want something real this time?" Wally asked seriously, all kidding gone from his voice.

"Yeah, I think that's what I want. But what if it's not what he wants?" Phillip sighed. "I know there are no guarantees. It's just that I never felt this way before. I've only kissed him, but every time I do, the world sort of stops." Phillip cut off the remainder of his thought as Mario strode over from the barn with David holding his arm. It was nice to see Mario happy.

"What are you two talking about, heads together like hens?" Mario asked teasingly.

"We're planning an exercise area for the cats," Wally said matter-of-factly, to Phillip's eternal gratitude.

"Cats? You mean there's another one already?" David asked, his eyes wide.

"Not yet, but a tiger is arriving in the next few days, and Phillip suggested we build an exercise area with gates to control access so both the cats can use it. We're going to start tomorrow—any volunteers?"

Mario looked at David and then back at Wally. "Looks like we're in."

"Me too," Phillip added.

"Then I'd better get to town before everything closes, and you," Wally said, turning to Phillip, "you need to get ready for your adventure in the wilds of Wyoming." Wally winked and hurried to his truck.

"You need help?" David asked.

Wally hung his head out the driver's window. "Won't say no."

David gave Mario a kiss before jogging to the passenger door. Climbing in, David slammed the door, and Wally started moving down the drive, waving as he disappeared in a cloud of dust.

"I've got some things to finish up," Mario said once the truck was out of sight, "but have fun tonight, and I'll see you tomorrow." Phillip caught the edge in the man's voice.

"You okay, Mario?" Phillip called, as the foreman started toward the barn.

"Yeah." He stopped, turning to Phillip. "It just feels a little strange having you here. Not that it's your fault or nothing. It just feels weird, I guess."

"Because you're with David?" Phillip asked.

"Yeah, I guess." Mario chewed a fingernail—Phillip knew Mario only did that when he was nervous.

Phillip didn't know what to say. Part of him felt secretly pleased that Mario was still affected by him, even in a roundabout way. "I saw you and David the other day. You both looked happy, and I think it's wonderful." Mario needed closure, and hell, so did he, for that matter. They'd been avoiding each other since he arrived. "I didn't come here expecting to get you back. We had a good time last summer, but what you have with David seems real." Mario smiled, big and bright, eyes shining. "See, you never smiled for me like that. And that's okay, because you deserve to be happy enough to smile like that."

"So do you, Phillip," Mario said, nodding softly as he turned back toward the barn. Phillip waited until Mario disappeared into the barn before leaping up the steps and into the house. After all, he had a camping trip to pack for.

Phillip went to his room, opening the dresser drawers, trying to figure out what to pack. Finally, saying to hell with it, he threw a change of clothes in a bag along with a sweatshirt in case it got cold. Hearing Wally's voice in his head, he threw in some supplies as well before carrying the bag to the living room. "Hey, Dakota," Phillip said, waving as he saw the big man emerge from his dad's room. "How's he doing?"

"Good. I'm going to bring Dad into the living room for the evening," Dakota said before disappearing into the bedroom. Phillip plopped onto the sofa, and a few minutes later, Dakota wheeled his dad next to the sofa, setting the brakes on his chair.

"Would you like a beer?" Phillip asked the wheelchair-bound man, and got as big a smile as possible in return.

"He really shouldn't have any, Phillip," Dakota scolded lightly.

"Kota," Phillip said, grinning as he got up, "your dad knows what he can and can't do." He opened the refrigerator door, getting out three beers. Phillip figured Dakota would argue less if he was included in their little beer party. Returning to the living room, Phillip handed one to Dakota and set a bottle on the table before opening Jefferson's and placing it in his hand. Opening his own, he flopped down on the sofa next to Dakota, happily waiting for his ride.

"He really shouldn't be drinking—it messes with his meds," Dakota said softly as he turned on the television, finding a baseball game for his dad.

"The last time I gave him one, he nursed it most of the evening, and I dumped at least half of it away," Phillip said in a low voice as he took a swig from the bottle. "He just wants to feel like a whole man every once in a while. But I won't give him any more if you really don't want me to."

Dakota bumped his shoulder, looking at him with a smile. "When did you get so smart?"

"I've always been smart. As I recall, the last couple times we were together, we were either occupied with something other than conversation, or there was a particular veterinarian who had you all tied in knots."

"I understand you're going camping," Jefferson said, his voice slurred a little more than usual.

"With Haven, yes." Phillip finished off his beer, setting the bottle on the table.

"He's nice, unlike that son of a bitch he has for a father." Jefferson's vehemence had Phillip looking at Dakota for some sort of explanation, but he just shrugged. Whatever was between those two, Dakota had no clue, and neither did Haven. Phillip couldn't help thinking that whatever it was, it must have been a humdinger of a fight for both men to carry the grudge that long.

"What is it with you and Haven's father, anyway?" Dakota asked, and Phillip found himself very interested.

At first Jefferson pretended not to hear, but when Dakota kept staring at his dad, the older man rolled his head toward him. "Don't wanna talk about it," Jefferson finally said, turning back to the television, sipping his beer, face hard as stone.

A truck pulling up outside made Phillip forget all about anything but Haven as he jumped up, looking out the window. "I'll see you tomorrow."

Jefferson raised his hand slightly as a goodbye. "You got your phone, just in case?" Dakota asked.

"Yes, Mother," Phillip answered, winking at Jefferson, who hooted slightly.

Grabbing his bag, he walked outside and down the steps, over to where Haven waited. Throwing the bag in the back, he climbed in the cab. "I just brought clothes. I wasn't sure if you needed anything."

"Nope, got everything we need in the back," Haven said with a smile, and Phillip leaned close, getting a light kiss before Haven put the truck in gear.

"Where are we going?" Phillip asked as Haven pulled out onto the road.

"Where we went after dinner."

"You mean Hump Hill?" Phillip had to ask, especially given the thoughts he'd been having about Haven for the past few days.

"It's a great spot, and it's not far away if something should happen," Haven explained as they rode, more like *flew*, over the country roads.

"Where did you tell your dad you were going?"

Haven looked across the seat, eyes clouding for a second. "I told him I was going camping. He asked why, and I said I needed to get away from him. We've barely talked to each other in days, not since we fought after you and Wally brought the calf over." Phillip nodded and listened. Haven had already told him about the fight. "But at least he's been helping on the ranch. Dad's pretty handy and knows a little about everything, so at least some of the things I never get time for have gotten done, like fixing the back door and running another water line to the barn. But I don't expect it to last." Haven sounded resigned, and Phillip didn't push it. He really didn't want to talk about Haven's dad, or anything else for that matter.

Sitting quietly, they rode for a few minutes more before pulling off the road and along a short drive. Even though it had been dark when he was here before, he remembered the view, and Phillip looked around him, remembering the landmarks Haven had pointed out—they looked so very different during the day.

Haven killed the engine and moved to get out, but Phillip was faster, sliding across the bench seat, touching him on the shoulder. When Haven turned toward him, Phillip leaned closer, hand sliding around the back of Haven's neck. "I've been looking forward to this for days," Phillip whispered before bringing their lips together. Haven's lips parted almost immediately, and Phillip loved how responsive he was. Small moans filled the cab of the truck, and Phillip deepened the kiss as Haven's arms wound around him, tugging him closer, using his weight to lean Phillip back on the seat. It wasn't long before Haven had Phillip prone beneath him, and Phillip was having the breath kissed out of him. "Where did you learn to kiss like that?" Phillip asked, gasping for air. He didn't wait for an answer before going for more from Haven's full lips.

"From you," Haven responded, grinning down at him, eyes clouded and heavy.

"But we only kissed a few times," Phillip moaned softly, arching as Haven kissed his neck.

"I learn fast," Haven retorted before cutting off further discussion with his lips, not that Phillip cared the least little bit. They kissed until the inside of the truck turned into a sauna, windows steamed up and both men sweaty. "We should set up before it gets dark," Haven told Phillip as he finally let him up.

Phillip's lips tingled, his back and legs a little stiff, along with another part—not that Phillip minded in the least. Haven opened his door and slid out, allowing Phillip to climb out as well.

Haven went around to the back of the truck. Phillip shut the door and joined him, peering into the bed. "Where's the tent?"

"Don't need one," Haven told him. "I brought pads and blankets. I thought we'd sleep under the stars back here." Haven turned to him, tugging on his lower lips with his teeth. "That's okay, isn't it?"

"It's wonderful," Phillip answered, taking the things that Haven handed to him.

"We shouldn't build a fire. Even with the recent rain, the ground's too dry to take any chances, so I brought a small grill and the things for a nice dinner." Haven pulled out a cooler, setting it and the Hibachi onto the ground. "Everything else can stay in the truck." Haven closed the tailgate and began setting up the grill.

"Is there anything I can do?"

"Why don't you get a couple beers out of the cooler. I'll light the grill and start dinner. We should eat. It'll be dark soon."

Phillip opened the lid of the cooler, pulling out two beers, twisting off the tops before handing one to Haven and staying out of his way. The man was a model of efficiency. It wasn't long before he had the grill lit and their bed all made up in the back of the truck. Then he returned to the grill, checking the heat before opening the cooler, pulling out a couple of steaks and laying them on the grill with a sear that made Phillip's mouth water.

"I only have paper plates," he said as he handed them to Phillip along with knives and forks. Not that it mattered in the least. Soon Phillip's mouth was filled with the most tender, juiciest cut of beef he'd ever tasted. Using the cooler as a table and sitting on the ground, they ate quietly, the twilight filled with the sounds of gustatory pleasure.

"Do you always cook like this?" Phillip looked down at his plate, wondering where his huge appetite had come from.

"Like what?" Haven asked innocently, but Phillip could tell Haven was just being modest. The man knew what he was doing around a grill—that was for sure.

Phillip swallowed his bite of heaven. "Like this…." He signaled down at his plate, which was now nearly empty. "That was the best steak I've ever eaten in my life." Phillip popped the last morsel into his mouth, chewing slowly, savoring the flavor on this tongue.

Haven beamed, and Phillip watched in the fading light as he finished off his as well. "It's the outdoors. It always makes the food taste better," Haven quipped, but Phillip could just see the pleased look on his face as the sun gave up the ghost, the last rays of the day slipping away. Phillip gathered the plates, throwing them and the empty bottles into the bag Haven had set out for trash. As night fully descended, Phillip could see nothing, and he listened as Haven moved around him. "Is there a light?" he asked softly.

"We don't need one," Haven answered, and Phillip felt warmth press against him, arms lifting him, guiding him. Phillip felt the truck against his back, heard the tailgate drop, then he was guided up and onto soft bedding. Phillip felt the truck move as Haven joined him, tugging him close. This time Phillip held back nothing, devouring Haven's lips as his hands roamed at will. Haven was strong, there was no doubt about it, and Phillip felt those muscles quiver beneath his touch.

The air around them still held the heat of the day, and Phillip slipped his hands beneath Haven's shirt, tugging it up and over his head, their kiss broken only by the fabric. Warm skin under his hands, the manly scent of work and sweat filling his nose, and the taste of Haven's lips all combined to drive Phillip nearly out of his mind with want, and he shuddered as Haven lifted his shirt. Phillip helped him get it off, and then their chests came together, skin against skin, with a sigh that reverberated in both their throats, the intensity increasing with each touch, each breath, each kiss.

"Phillip," Haven said as his hands stopped moving, lips lifting away, "is this okay? I mean, am I okay?"

"What?" Phillip didn't understand at all. "You're more than okay. Is something wrong?" Phillip struggled to a seated position, leaning against the side of the truck bed.

"No. It's just that I've never done anything like this before, and…." Haven's voice became soft, and Phillip could hear his insecurity when he said, "What if I'm no good?"

Phillip wanted to laugh. His body still hummed, and all they'd done was kiss and remove their shirts. *No good?* Haven had him so worked up he thought he'd explode. "I don't think you need to worry about that." Phillip moved slowly toward Haven's voice. "You don't have to do anything you don't want, and whatever you do will be perfect. You can't do anything wrong as long as you do it with feeling." Phillip felt Haven's leg, finding his bearings, hand trailing along Haven's chest and up his neck. Lips followed his fingers, zeroing in on Haven's, kissing again—this time slow, letting the pleasure build.

"You taste good," Haven said softly, returning the kisses.

"So do you." Phillip kissed his way down Haven's neck to his shoulder, kissing the small dip at the base of his neck. "You taste like outdoors and sunshine," Phillip said softly as he trailed his lips down Haven's chest, hearing a soft moan as he licked across a small, pert nipple.

"Philly," Haven said softly when Phillip sucked lightly, shoving his chest forward, begging for more. And Phillip obliged, circling his tongue around the tiny bud, sucking and licking first one, then the other. Easing Haven onto the bedding, Phillip could just make out his silhouette in the light from the moon and stars. He found Haven's lips, kissing again as he ran his hands over the younger man's smooth skin.

"We've got all night, Haven, and I want to make this special," Phillip whispered softly, tongue trailing down Haven's throat. "I want to taste you." Phillip licked a trail first to one nipple, then the other, nipping lightly at the salty sweet skin. "Feel you," he said, fingers trailing along behind, feeling the ripple of each muscle, the hitch in Haven's breath.

"Philly, what are you doing to me?" Haven asked in a squeaky voice, shaking beneath him, and Phillip smiled, kissing his way down Haven's quivering belly, feeling it jump with every touch. At his belt, Phillip unfastened the buckle, slipping the leather out of its loops. Haven's breath caught when Phillip opened the catch on his jeans, sliding his zipper down before parting the fabric.

Phillip could see nothing, but he didn't have to. The catch in Haven's breath, and the shake in his legs, told him everything he needed to know. Slowly, listening to every one of Haven's reactions, Phillip slid his fingers lightly over Haven's cotton-encased erection. The whimper he received from the big man sounded like the grandest symphony he'd ever heard.

"Philly," Haven cried softly.

Phillip soothed his hand up Haven's stomach, rubbing small circles. "Just taking my time." He could tell Haven was trying to sit up so he could see, or at least try to. "Lay back and feel, Haven. That's all you need to do, just feel." This was his young lover's first experience, and it was going to be absolutely mind-blowing if Phillip had anything to say about it.

Slipping his fingers beneath the elastic, he ran them along Haven's stomach, teasing the cotton lower, kissing the quivering skin as he went. When he thought Haven could take no more, he pulled the elastic lower and off, sliding both the underwear and Haven's jeans off his legs. Able to see nothing, he slid his hands back up Haven's calves, then his thighs, before sliding his fingers along Haven's sizable erection. As Phillip's fingers encircled it, he felt Haven's hips buck almost immediately.

Stroking lightly, he brought their lips together and felt Haven trying to work his pants off. "I want to feel you, Phillip." Sitting on the bedding, Phillip stripped himself of his remaining clothing before straddling Haven and lying on top of him. Arms encircled him almost immediately, hugging him tight as their hips rocked lightly, cocks sliding past each other.

With every movement, Phillip could hear Haven gasp and moan, hips moving faster, breath becoming erratic. Phillip himself could barely breathe. Wherever his skin touched Haven's, it seemed to tingle—legs, chest, hands, feet. Pressure built fast, Haven gripping him tight, breath hitching. He could feel Haven's impending explosion, and with a cry that flew across the range, Haven came between them, gasping for breath as he called Phillip's name.

Phillip had never had anyone call his name like that—he could almost hear it echoing over the land as his own climax barreled into him, and he added his release to Haven's, gripping the man so tight he was afraid he might have left bruises. Phillip lay where he was, breathing hard, Haven's hands stroking his back.

"Was that okay?" Haven sounded tentative.

"It was," Phillip said, heaving a breath, "amazing."

"You're not disappointed that we didn't…." Haven became quiet, and Phillip listened intently, waiting for Haven to finish his thought. "You know, fuck."

Phillip stroked a hand along Haven's cheek. "Making love doesn't always involve intercourse. There are so many ways to make love, and what we did was only one of them." And Phillip wanted to show each and every one of those ways to Haven, if it took the rest of his life.

"Is that what we did, made love?" Haven sounded rather pleased.

"I hope so, otherwise, when we do make love, you'll probably kill me," Phillip said, holding Haven close before finding his lips again, kissing the man hard. He didn't want to wonder if this meant more to him than it did to Haven. Phillip couldn't help how he felt, and if Haven didn't feel the same way, Phillip would have to live with that. The feel of a towel being pressed into his hand pulled him out of his thoughts. Wiping them both off, Phillip settled onto the bedding, resting his head on Haven's shoulder, both of them peering up at the stars.

"They're beautiful tonight," Haven said softly, a hand stroking over Phillip's side. "Is it me or do they seem brighter?" Phillip smiled his answer, snuggling closer as the night air took on a slight chill. "I just have one question."

"Okay...?" Phillip felt Haven moving around and then a blanket settled over the both of them.

"Can we do that again in the morning?" Haven's hand slipped into his.

Phillip smiled. "I hope so." He moved closer to Haven, and they watched together as a streak of light shot across the sky. Haven rolled onto his side, capturing Phillip's lips. Together they watched the stars and talked softly of the things new lovers do, until they both drifted off, the stars keeping watch.

## Chapter Seven

HAVEN didn't sleep well. There was no possible way. Every time he moved he felt Phillip next to him, smelled his scent, or heard him breathing. "Haven." Phillip rolled over, and Haven felt a hand slide over his chest. "I take it you can't sleep either."

"Nope." Haven yawned as he squirmed on top of Phillip, feeling the other man's excitement slide along his.

"Then I want you to lie on your back for me."

"Why?" Haven asked, just able to make out the slight glimmer of Phillip's eyes. Haven waited, but didn't get an answer verbally. Instead, he felt Phillip's hands slide down his back and over his butt. Then with surprising speed, Haven found himself on his back with Phillip on top of him. He grunted in surprise and heard Phillip chuckle lightly before Phillip's tongue slid around a nipple and Haven was gone, lost in an instant haze of desire.

"What do you want, Haven?" Phillip asked, breath sliding along wet skin, raising goose bumps in the cool night air.

"I don't know," Haven whined softly as Phillip continued working his nipple with those amazing lips. God, he loved that. Phillip seemed to know just how to touch him.

"Haven," Phillip said softly, "you must have fantasized about this for years. When you closed your eyes at night and dreamed of your first time, what did you dream of?" Haven swallowed and felt his body stiffen. There was no way he was going to tell Phillip about that. The man would think he was just too freaky. "Haven, we all have little fantasies that really turn us on, what's yours?" The lips stopped moving, and Haven could feel Phillip's eyes on him, even though it was pitch black and he could see nothing.

"I… I… no, you'll think it's too weird." Haven let his head fall back against the cold pillow, feeling Phillip against his skin, unmoving… waiting. "I always pictured a man, big and strong, who held me down and did things to me," Haven confessed, and he felt himself blush at the admission.

"You imagined yourself held down?" He heard Phillip's voice and felt Phillip's hands slide along his arms, capturing his wrists. "Like this?"

"Uh-huh, but he usually tied my hands," Haven admitted, feeling the heat rush to his groin.

"It's too soon for that. You need to learn what things mean, but we can start with something else. Something easy."

"Okay, what do I do?" Haven could feel his excitement ramp up as Phillip's hands tightened their grip.

"I want you to put your hands over your head. Do you feel the metal from the truck bed?"

"Yes," Haven groaned softly. "I can feel it."

"I want you to put the back of your hands against the metal and leave them there," Phillip said, his voice becoming slightly harder, more commanding. "Don't remove them unless I tell you."

"Okay." Haven complied, the cool metal pressing against his knuckles. Phillip's hands slid back down his arms and along his side. Haven squirmed at the slight tickle, but suppressed the urge to remove his hands to fend them off.

"Very good," Phillip said, and Haven felt lips against his skin, hot and wet, tongue licking trails over his nipples and down to his belly button. Then Phillip lifted himself away, the night air caressing Haven's skin, the truck still. All Haven could hear was Phillip's breathing, and his entire body tensed, wondering where the sensation would appear.

Haven jumped as Phillip's tongue slid along his inner thigh. He almost pulled his hands away from the sheer surprise, but stopped himself just in time. "Phillip, you startled me."

"I know. That was the idea. I needed to know if you were listening, and you were. Your hands stayed on the metal, didn't they?"

"Uh-huh," Haven answered as Phillip's tongue moved a little higher. "Are you gonna…?"

Phillip's tongue and lips stopped, again everything became still, the only sound his own breathing. Haven's cock throbbed against his stomach, and he wanted to thrust his hips forward to see where Phillip was, but a hand slid along his leg and up, up, up, ghosting across the indentation of his hip, barely missing his cock. The groan he let out filled the night, and he heard Phillip chuckle. "Before, I asked you what you wanted, and you said you didn't know—do you now?"

"Yes," Haven whined loudly. "I want your lips on me." He gasped, waiting. Then he felt Phillip's lips just brush along his shaft ever so lightly. He bucked forward and they disappeared. Haven stilled and the lips returned, warm and wet, sliding over him. Haven clenched his eyes closed, body tensing as he gave himself over to the sensation, afraid to move or Phillip would stop.

"There, you get it," Phillip said softly, warm air blowing over wet skin, making Haven's cock jump against his belly. "This is about you feeling and giving yourself over for a while. No worries, nothing but feeling." The sensation intensified, and Haven felt Phillip's lips move toward the head, tongue teasing the sweet spot before sliding away. Haven felt himself whine, and Phillip moved upward again, lips taking him in. Haven stilled, not daring to move, hoping Phillip would take him deeper, but the lips moved away again.

"Phillip, you're being mean," Haven whined, pressing his hands back against the metal.

"No. I'm teaching control," Phillip corrected, and he did it again. Haven nearly swore but stopped himself and was rewarded when

Phillip's lips closed over him, mouth sucking him deeper, and Haven let out a satisfied sigh that surprised even him.

"Yes," Haven cried as Phillip took him deep, sucking hard, hands slipping beneath him. "Oh God, yes!" Haven felt Phillip's hands cup his butt, fingers gripping his cheeks, as Phillip's lips slid along his shaft. Everything else around him fell away. The crickets became silent, the stars disappeared, the chill from the metal fell away as Haven's entire consciousness narrowed to what Phillip was doing to his body. "Philly!" Haven cried out, and the lips slipped away from him.

"No one calls me Philly," Phillip said firmly. "That's a cream cheese, not your lover. You can call me Phillip or sir."

Haven swallowed and found himself nodding vigorously, forgetting that Philip couldn't see him. "Okay, Phillip." There was no way he was calling his lover sir. That was just too creepy and weird for him.

The lips sank around him again, and Haven's breath whooshed from his lungs. He felt Phillip's hands press against his butt, and he thrust a little. When Phillip sucked harder, Haven figured Phillip had given him permission and he thrust harder. Soon he thrust with abandon, completely lost in the sensation, his mind clouded in a haze of passion. "Phillip," he whimpered, trying to give his lover warning before he exploded, buried deep in Philip's throat, body throbbing.

HAVEN opened his eyes, but could see nothing. Coming back to himself, he felt Phillip's hand on his belly, rubbing slowly. "Are you okay? You didn't say anything or move for the longest time."

"You blew my mind," Haven answered. "Umm, can I move my hands now?"

"Yes, but put them at your sides," Phillip answered softly in the darkness. Then he felt Phillip's lips on his, kissing hard, his mouth and tongue being devoured. "What about you? Can I"—Haven felt himself swallow—"return the favor?"

"Are you sure?"

"God, yes," Haven answered after Phillip had kissed him again.

"Then leave your hands at your side," Phillip said softly, and Haven felt Phillip straddle him as a finger slid past his lips. Haven sucked it deep and heard Phillip moan softly before scooting forward. Haven felt Phillip's cock against his lips and opened his mouth. Phillip slid forward just a little, and Haven sucked, his mouth exploding with Phillip's unique flavor. Damn, he wanted more, and he began sucking harder. He felt Phillip's hand on his cheek and slowed down. "That's better. Take your time." Phillip moved a little closer, and Haven felt him begin to move, slowly rocking back and forth, his lover's cock sliding over his tongue.

Haven felt his body react, his dick already hard again, bouncing against his stomach. He felt Phillip twist a little and then fingers closed around him, stroking as Phillip thrust back and forth. Haven sucked with increasing ferocity, taking Phillip as deep as he'd let him. Relaxing his throat, he took all he could get for just a second before backing away and trying again. "Haven," he heard Phillip groan, and he smiled around the cock in his mouth, desperately wanting to give Phillip the same pleasure he'd received.

Already Haven could feel Phillip driving him toward another release, and Phillip's moans filled the night around them. Haven exploded into the tight ring of Phillip's fingers as Phillip stilled, climaxing hard. Haven swallowed, and then again, letting the intense flavor settle on his tongue before taking all he could.

Slowly, Phillip pulled out, and Haven heard him gasping for breath, lying down next to him. Haven rolled onto his side, tugging Phillip close, heedless of any mess, and kissing him hard. "Was that as good as your fantasy?" Phillip asked, and Haven knew he was smiling.

"Much better than anything I could imagine," Haven responded as he felt Phillip stroke his cheek before their lips found each other's.

Phillip tugged the blanket back over them, and this time Haven found himself easily drifting into a deep, happy sleep with Phillip holding him tight.


RICH dreams of loving and being loved filled his mind, but there was just one thing—*why was there a truck engine and brakes squealing in his dream? And why in the hell was Dakota suddenly in his bedroom, telling him to get up?* His shoulder being shaken finally pulled him out of his dream, and he opened his eyes to see Dakota standing next to the truck. "Haven, you need to get up. You, too, Phillip." At first he thought Dakota might be playing a joke on them, but the man's voice didn't carry the least bit of humor. In fact, its nervous edge had Haven almost instantly afraid.

"Why are you here? What's wrong?" Haven asked as he sat up, Phillip stirring next to him.

"You both need to get dressed and back to our place as soon as possible," Dakota said, the tone of his voice enough to have Haven searching for his clothes.

"Is everyone okay?" Haven asked, but Dakota simply walked back toward his truck.

"I'll explain everything I can back at the house." The look Dakota gave him sent a chill down his spine. Something had happened, and he almost jumped out of the truck, naked or not, and demanded an answer.

Instead, Haven watched as Dakota climbed into his truck, then the engine started, and he was gone. As soon as he was out of sight, Haven slipped out from under the covers, pulling on his clothes, heart pounding a mile a minute.

"It'll be okay, Haven," Phillip said from next to him, a hand touching his shoulder.

"Did you see the way he looked at me? It's something bad. I know it." He finished dressing, pulling on his boots before jumping down out of the truck. "Would you roll up the bedding?" he asked Phillip, without even looking to see if he'd finished dressing. Dumping the cold coals from the grill, Haven gathered everything from last night, and once the bedding was rolled away, began hoisting everything into the truck. With every movement, a new surge of adrenaline coursed through him, and he moved faster and faster. By the time they were all packed up, his legs were shaking.

"Haven, it's really going to be okay. Do you want me to drive?" Phillip asked, and without thinking, Haven handed him the keys. Haven climbed into the truck, and Phillip started the engine before backing away and onto the small country road.

Phillip seemed to remember the route they'd taken the night before, because soon they pulled into Dakota's. Getting out, Haven hurried up the steps and inside, with Phillip right behind him. Wally and Dakota sat on the sofa, Dakota looking furious and Wally as white as a sheet. But it was Sheriff Harker who caught his attention as he got up from one of the chairs.

"Sheriff, what's going on?" Haven asked, looking around the room.

"Haven, son, I have some bad news," the sheriff started, and Haven felt Phillip's hands on his shoulders. "Your dad was found dead this morning. He'd been crushed by his horse."

Haven thought his knees would give out, but somehow he remained standing. He felt Phillip guide him toward a chair. "How did this happen?" Haven asked, but whatever answer was given, he didn't hear it. Yes, the man was a bigot and they didn't always see eye to eye, but he was still his father and regardless of other things, Haven had loved the man.

"Haven," Dakota said as he stood in front of his chair. "I know this is hard for you and is going to get harder, but do you know why your father was on a horse in the middle of the night?"

Haven forced his mind to focus. "What? He was what?"

Sheriff Harker stepped forward, ushering Dakota back to his seat. "Haven," the huge man began, his voice soft and understanding. "We're still trying to piece things together, and the coroner hasn't provided a time of death yet, but it seems your father was on horseback when the horse stepped into a hole and broke its leg. He landed on top of your father."

Haven fought to breathe. He could hardly believe this was happening. "Mario found him this morning," Dakota added. "Wally put down the horse."

Haven watched dumbfounded as Wally walked over to him. "I'm sorry, Haven. He was riding Jake."

Haven looked blankly around the room, seeing nothing, trying to listen to what was being said, but hearing nothing more. His dad was dead. The horse that had been his friend and near constant companion for almost ten years was also dead. "Does Kade know?"

"We've told no one yet. There's still a lot we don't know," the sheriff explained. "Had your dad planned to go out?" Haven shook his head. "Was riding at night something he normally did?" Haven shook his head again.

"Dad hasn't done a lot of riding in the last couple of years," Haven answered, his mind swimming, trying to develop some sort of explanation for what happened, but unable to. Closing his eyes, Haven tried to block out everything, hoping to somehow press the reset button.

"I think you need to give him some time to process all this," Haven heard Phillip say from behind him.

"We need some answers," the sheriff said.

"No, you don't. Haven and I were camping together last night. He wasn't home and most likely hadn't seen his dad since early evening when he picked me up here. Dakota was with me when Haven's truck arrived."

"There are things he may be able to tell us if he'll answer some questions," the sheriff said rather forcefully, and Haven opened his eyes.

"Look," Haven heard Phillip say, the hands on his shoulder tightening, "this was an accident, correct?" Haven saw the sheriff nod. "Then find out what you can and come back. He's not going anywhere except maybe back to the ranch." Haven felt Phillip's hand slip away and then he found himself staring into Phillip's eyes. "It's going to be okay. We're all here for you."

Haven nodded slowly, his mind starting to function again. "I don't know why my dad did most of the things he did," Haven said. "Please find out what you can."

"I will, Haven. I'll contact you later today when I have something else." The sheriff left, the floor creaking as he walked out of the room, the door closing quietly behind him.

Haven saw all of them looking around the room at each other with equally confused looks. Wally seemed to be the first to recover. "I think we need something to eat."

Haven wasn't so sure what he needed right now, but food didn't rank high on his list. "Do you think they'll let me see him?"

"I'm sure they will," Phillip answered. "Don't worry about it right now. The sheriff needs to figure out what happened."

"Why? If it was an accident, why do they need to investigate like this?" Haven looked to Phillip and then Dakota, hoping for something to make sense.

"Haven," Dakota said softly, leaning forward in his chair, "they need to investigate because your father died on our land. He wasn't at home. He was on my East Range riding your horse."

Haven felt as if shock after shock were piling up on him. *Could his father have cut the fences and was then trying to frame him for it?*

"Come on in and get something to eat," Wally said walking in from the kitchen. Dakota got up and left the room. Haven saw Phillip walk into the kitchen, but he didn't move. He couldn't. His feet felt numb and his legs didn't seem to want to work. "Haven, sweetheart," Wally said from next to him, "you need to eat." Wally touched his arm, and Haven lifted himself out of the chair. Wally guided him into the kitchen and down onto one of the chairs.

A plate appeared in front of him, but Haven ignored it. "What am I going to do?"

"You don't have to do anything until you're ready," Dakota answered softly. "Once you've eaten, we'll take you home so you can get your things and talk to Kade. He's a good man. He can run things for a few days for you." Haven nodded absently, picking up a fork, taking a small bite of egg before setting the fork down again. His stomach rebelled at eating anything. "You should stay with friends for a few days," Dakota added, and Haven looked around the room, confused and not really able to figure out what was going on. "You're welcome to stay here, if you like. We'd be happy to have you, but if you'd rather go somewhere else, that's perfectly okay as well."

Haven had no idea what to do or where to go. The thought of going home was overwhelming. He knew he could go to Kade's. But their place was small and....

"It's okay, Haven," Phillip said soothingly from next to him. "Eat if you want, and we'll take you home. You can stay with me."

Haven nodded and ate another bite before pushing the plate away and sitting, not paying attention to much as the others ate. Dishes were cleared, and Phillip took his arm. "Dakota and I will take you home."

Haven got up and blankly followed them out of the house and to Dakota's truck. Getting in, he sat in the middle as Dakota drove up the street, turning into their... his driveway. Kade met the truck, and from the look on his face, it was obvious that he already knew what had happened. "Is there anything I can do?"

"Haven's going to stay with us for a few days. Can you take care of things here?" Dakota asked as Haven got out of the truck and led Phillip up the front steps and into the house. He walked through the quiet rooms and to his bedroom.

"There's a bag in the closet," he said quietly and heard the door slide. Opening his drawers, Haven transferred some clothes into his bag before closing it. Making a stop in the bathroom, he grabbed his travel kit and placed some things inside before meeting Phillip and Dakota in the living room.

"Kade will take care of things, and I told him to call if he needs anything. I can send one of my men to help."

"Thanks, Dakota," Haven said, looking around the house he'd spent his whole life in and yet now it felt completely different. "I'm alone," he whispered to himself, realizing for the first time in his life that there was no one else left—he was it. Haven might have complained about the way his dad acted, but he always knew his dad was taking care of things, and him.

"Let's go," Phillip said softly, taking Haven's hand, fingers lacing with his, and Haven felt Phillip's strength. Nodding slowly, he let his gaze slip away from the room, and followed Dakota out the door, Phillip still holding his hand.

Haven rode back to Dakota's in silence, wondering what he was going to do. Stepping back into Dakota's living room, he found Jefferson sitting quietly near the sofa, the television off. Haven sat on the sofa, his thoughts again sinking inward. Normally, he'd go riding when he felt lost and unsure, but that wasn't possible right now. Haven felt the tears threaten for the first time.

"It's okay," Jefferson said to him, a hand touching his, and Haven saw Jefferson reaching out to him.

"No, it's not," Haven argued, wiping his eyes.

"Yes, it is. It's okay to cry. He was your dad," Jefferson said softly, watching him.

The funny thing was that as Haven fought back the tears, he realized that right now, he was feeling the loss of Jake more keenly than he was the death of his own father. *What kind of person did that make him?*

Phillip sat down next to him, setting a soda on the table. Haven looked into those brown eyes and felt arms tug him close. Haven returned the hug and gave in to his grief, letting the tears come. Burying his face against Phillip's shoulder, Haven let go of his doubts and control, giving his emotions free rein, and grieved. Haven cried for his dad, for Jake, and even for himself. How long he held on to Phillip he wasn't really sure, but by the time he lifted his head, the wet spot on Phillip's shirt had gotten quite large.

In the afternoon, Haven let Phillip talk him into going for a walk. Phillip led him along one of the trails behind the house. They stopped at Schian's enclosure, and Haven watched the lion pace around the fence that lined the perimeter, head down, making no sound. Everything felt weird, like the world seemed flat and had lost a bit of its color.

Pounding and banging caught his attention, and Haven wandered over to where the guys were building Wally's exercise enclosure. In the warm air, Haven slipped off his shirt, setting it aside, and pitched in to help.

"It's okay, Haven," Wally said softly as he steadied one of the uprights, Dakota driving it into the ground with a handheld post driver. Without saying anything, Haven looked to Dakota, who stepped aside, and Haven took over the weighted collar. Lifting the weight, he drove the metal pole into the ground. Doing something felt good and helped clear his mind. Holes had been dug around the perimeter. Moving to the next one, Philip held the pole as Haven drove it deep. All afternoon, Haven worked. Others offered to relieve him, but Haven brushed them off, driving pole after pole into the ground, waiting for concrete to be poured around the base and then moving to the next one. He felt like a machine, and as long as he did, he could keep the emotions that threatened to surface again at bay. "Haven." Wally's voice cut through his hazy thoughts, and Haven stopped what he was doing. "That's enough for today." Wally touched his arm, and he let his hands slip away from the post driver. "You've driven every post we have. I think we're good."

Haven nodded and looked around. All the posts had been driven and cemented, holes filled, and the upper poles attached almost all the way around. "Sorry, I guess I got carried away."

"Let's go inside," Wally said, and Haven found Phillip standing next to him. The man had never been far away the entire day, and Haven was grateful. "We need to get some dinner, and Phillip can rub some lotion into your shoulders. They're going to really hurt tomorrow."

Haven didn't really care. For hours he'd been able to forget things temporarily and think about nothing. Phillip took his arm as they walked back toward the house, and Haven looked at him, smiling a smile he didn't really feel.

Wally made dinner, which Haven ate, but didn't actually taste. As they were finishing, Haven heard a knock on the door, and Dakota got up to answer it, returning with the sheriff in tow. "How are you holding up, Haven?"

"As well as can be expected, I guess," Haven answered as the sheriff sat down next to him. Haven noticed that Wally stood up, going to work in the kitchen until his phone rang and he rushed out to his truck.

"I have a few things I need to discuss with you," Sheriff Harker said, placing his hands on the table, his voice steady and reassuring. "We've determined your father's time of death, and unfortunately, it raises more questions than it answers. You father died between midnight and one a.m. last night. What we don't know is what he was doing on a horse at that time of night."

"On Dakota's land," Haven finished. "I wish I knew, Sheriff. We've had fences cut over the last week. Part of Dakota's herd got into our range, and a few nights ago someone cut part of the north fence and a calf got caught in the loose wire. None of this makes any sense to me at all. Yes, I know Dad and Mr. Holden didn't get along, but why he was on their land in the middle of the night has me stumped." Haven lifted his gaze to the sheriff. "What am I supposed to do with my dad's body?" Haven's thoughts skipped all around.

"I'll have someone from the funeral home call you in the morning. They can handle everything for you," Sheriff Harker explained gently. "I know there's a lot to think about, but don't worry about it right now. There are people to help you."

"Thanks," Haven said softly as the sheriff got up to leave.

"Do you know what happened to Jake?" Haven could barely think of his horse.

"Wally took care of everything when we called him this morning," the sheriff explained. "I'll stop by tomorrow to make sure everything's okay, and please don't hesitate to call if we can help." The sheriff said something to Dakota and then left.

"Was it Wally who had to put Jake down?" Haven asked, and Dakota nodded once. "Where is he?"

"After Wally put him down, we couldn't find you right away." Haven nodded. "So instead of having him carted away, we buried him near the large tree just outside the south range, where your property meets ours. I hope you don't mind, but we had to make a decision fast."

Haven didn't mind. He knew just where Dakota meant, and smiled. It was a good place for Jake. Haven made a note to go out there tomorrow. Getting up from the table, Haven wandered into the living room, yawning as he sat numbly on the sofa. Phillip followed him in, and they sat together with Dakota's dad, talking and watching baseball.

"Haven," Phillip said softly, and Haven realized he'd nearly fallen asleep, leaning against Phillip. "You should go to bed."

Haven nodded and got up, walking blankly through the house. Thankfully, Phillip guided him into his bedroom. Getting undressed, Haven climbed beneath the crisp covers. "Where are you going?" he asked Phillip when he saw him leaving the room.

"I'll sleep on the couch for tonight."

"Why?" Haven asked, a lump forming in his throat, tears threatening to well in his eyes.

"I didn't want you to think you had to," Phillip responded softly as he moved closer. "You need to rest, and I don't want to keep you up or anything."

Haven didn't want to be alone, and he found himself clinging to Phillip until Phillip slipped out of his clothes and got in bed with him, turning off the light. Haven held him close, wondering for a second how he'd gotten so close to Phillip in just a few days, and why he felt he'd be lost without him.

"Lay on your stomach," Phillip told him, and Haven rolled over. Phillip's hands slid along his shoulders, which had already started to ache from the exertion of the afternoon. Phillip's hands slid over his skin, soothing away the ache in his muscles and touching the ache inside. Haven knew nothing was going to make it go away totally except time, but Phillip's hands helped, and when Phillip lay down next to him in the air-conditioned room, tugging him close, Haven tried his best to let go of what he could.

## Chapter Eight

PHILLIP woke, dragging his eyes open as the first sounds in the house roused him from sleep. Not that he'd gotten much. Haven had tossed most of the night, alternating between clutching at him and then moving away, only to talk in his sleep. Looking at his bed partner, eyes closed, finally still and appearing to be resting peacefully, Phillip lay on the mattress afraid to move. Yesterday had been hard on Haven, losing his dad and all, and Phillip wanted to let him sleep, because he figured the young man was going to have another tough day today.

The door to the bedroom cracked open, and Wally's head appeared around it. Wally smiled slightly before backing away, the door closing again without so much as a click. Phillip stayed where he was even though his body craved coffee in the worst way. The door opened again, and Wally walked in, setting a mug on the bedside table before leaving again. *Damn, he owed the man big time for that.* Moving a little at a time, Phillip sat up, sipping his coffee, thinking as he stared at the cream walls. Phillip knew he could only hide here for so long. There were things he needed to do. It wasn't as though he had a job to go back to, but he felt like he was hiding, staying away from his life because it was easier than going out and fixing what was wrong. Haven rolled over, an arm sliding over his hips, and damned if Phillip couldn't feel his body react in an instant, suppressing the urge to moan as Haven's arm slid against his erection. He'd been hard most of the night. Every time he'd breathed in Haven's scent, his dick would throb, which would be fine under normal circumstances, but not with someone grieving. Turning to look, he saw Haven's face, relaxed and calm, lips slightly parted, eyes closed, hair half falling into his eyes. He looked so young and sweet. Phillip resisted the urge to stroke, sipping quietly from his mug instead.

Finishing his coffee, Phillip set the mug on the nightstand, and Haven shifted in his sleep, rolling onto his side and away from him. Gingerly, Phillip got out of bed. Grabbing pants and a shirt from the dresser, he tiptoed out of the room, peering back at Haven's sleeping form one last time before closing the door. Phillip dressed in the hallway, pulling on his pants and tugging the shirt over his head before walking toward the heavenly scents coming from the kitchen. Wally stood at the stove. "Morning," Phillip whispered as if Haven were still in the room next to him. "Where's Dakota?"

"He's out working already with Bucky and Mario," Wally answered, yawning. "Sorry, I was on a call most of the night. The horse is going to be fine, thank God, but it was touch and go for a while." Wally yawned again and this time made no effort to cover it. "They're beautiful creatures, strong and fragile at the same time. We walked the colicky animal for hours. I was beginning to think she had an obstruction, but...." Blessedly, Wally stopped when Phillip began to shake his head. "Sorry, I'm used to telling all this to Dakota. I forget how squeamish you are about this stuff."

"It's okay, just too early," Phillip grunted, pouring another mug of wakeup juice before sitting at the table. "I'm thinking I should be heading home soon." Phillip peered up at Wally, who turned his attention back to the stove and said nothing. "I need to get my job situation straightened out. It's a hell of a time to be unemployed."

A bang had Phillip jumping nearly out of his seat. "You're a piece of work, you know that?" Glaring daggers at him, Wally pulled his pan off the heat.

"What?" Phillip asked, definitely confused.

"You're doing it again. The going gets tough or even slightly serious, and you're gone." Wally returned to his cooking. "Don't think for one second I didn't see the longing looks you gave Mario when you first arrived. You may be able to fool yourself into believing you weren't hurt that he'd moved on, but you weren't fooling me. You were hoping you could pick up where you two left off." Wally stepped closer, and Phillip leaned back in the chair. "Is that what you're doing with Haven? Some quickie substitution for Mario?"

"No," Phillip said as he swallowed, wondering what had gotten into his friend.

"Then what is it? Every time someone gets close, you back away. With Dakota and Mario, you hid behind the 'it's only vacation fun' excuse. Thankfully that worked for you with Dakota, because he's mine." Wally gave him a look that chilled him to the bone for just a second. "But you lost Mario because of it, and you're going to lose Haven, too, if you pull that crap again." Wally looked toward the bedroom, and Phillip saw some of the intensity slip from his expression. "Sorry, I shouldn't lecture. It's your life, not mine."

"Maybe you're right, but guys usually find out I'm a good time and then move on."

"Do they? Or is it you who moves on?" Wally asked as he went back to the stove. "You can't expect to do the same things you always did and get a different result."

Phillip lifted his coffee mug, stopping it halfway to his lips. *Was Wally right? God knows he'd been acting the same as he always did around Haven, but there was something different this time.* "What if it doesn't work out?"

Wally turned off the stove, setting the pan aside. "Let me ask you this: what if it does?" Wally said nothing more, but looked back at him for a few seconds before walking to the front door. Phillip didn't hear him call, but he soon returned with Dakota, Mario, and David right behind him. A soft knock followed, and Dakota got up, talking quietly in the next room before Jefferson's nurse made her way down the hall. Dakota returned and they ate quietly, talking in whispers until Phillip heard a door open down the hall.

Haven walked into the kitchen looking like he'd at least slept a little. "Would you like some breakfast?" Wally asked, and Haven shook his head as he sat in one of the empty chairs.

"Did you sleep?" Mario asked as he reached for the coffee, pouring a mug for Haven before refilling his own.

"Some, I guess," Haven replied into his coffee without picking it up, looking blankly around the table. "I guess I should get ready. There's all kinds of stuff to get done." Haven got up, leaving his mug, shuffling back down the hallway. Phillip gulped the last of his coffee before getting up himself, hurrying after him.

"Go ahead and get cleaned up. I'll meet you in the living room, if you want me to go with you, that is," Phillip said hurriedly, adding the last part, realizing he'd assumed Haven would want him to go along.

"You don't have to," Haven replied softly before opening the bedroom door.

"I know, and if you want to go alone, I'll understand." It was truly Haven's decision, but in a funny way Phillip knew he'd feel hurt if Haven didn't want him to go. The man needed someone, and Phillip hoped he'd want him with him.

Haven nodded his head. "Thanks." The bedroom door closed, and a few minutes later, Haven padded across the hall to the bathroom, carrying his things in a bundle, and Phillip used that opportunity to change his clothes. Once Haven returned, Phillip used the bathroom before waiting in the living room. Haven joined him a few minutes later before walking outside.

Phillip heard Wally walk into the room, smiling at him. "There's nothing sexier than someone who trusts you when they're vulnerable."

Phillip didn't say anything as he made sure he had everything he'd need. "Thanks," Phillip said, kissing his friend on the cheek. "You were right," he said before walking outside to Haven's truck.


THE morning was hard on Phillip and even harder on Haven. Visiting the funeral home brought back memories for Phillip of making the arrangements for his own father's funeral a few years earlier. But Phillip did his best not to dwell on those memories, particularly after seeing the agonizing time Haven was having making the arrangements for his dad's service. Haven had no idea about his father's wishes and just couldn't seem to decide what to do. "What is it you want?" Phillip asked him when the funeral director left the room for a few minutes to allow them to decide on a coffin. "Funerals are a chance for the living to say goodbye."

Haven looked at him, damn near in tears. "I want him buried on the ranch, but they say that's not that easy."

"There is another option," Phillip said softly. "You can have him cremated. Then you can spread his ashes wherever you want them."

The funeral director came back in the room. "Have you decided?"

Haven looked around the room at all the choices, and Philip saw the moment he decided. Haven's jaw became firm and his eyes cleared. "Yes." Even his voice seemed more confident. "I'd like to have him cremated and then a memorial service at the church." Haven looked at the urns standing on pedestals in the corner. "And I'd like that container for his ashes," he said as he pointed out a brushed bronze urn.

"Oh." The man looked surprised for a split second and then his calm expression returned. "We'll contact the minister and arrange for him to meet with you." Haven nodded and they left the room. After making the rest of the arrangements, Phillip followed Haven outside. He would have liked to see the sun to clear away the clouds from his spirit, but Mother Nature seemed to be feeling as gloomy as Haven, the clouds doing their best to touch the ground.

"Can we visit Jake?" Haven asked as they climbed into the truck.

"Of course." Phillip answered and pulled out his phone, calling the ranch to let them know they were on the way back and to ask Dakota if they could borrow one of the ATVs.

Half an hour later, in spite of the gloom and mist, Phillip found himself on an ATV behind Haven, bouncing across the range. As they approached a huge old tree, Haven slowed, the gash in the earth plain to see. Stopping the vehicle, Haven killed the engine and climbed off. Phillip stayed behind, figuring Haven would want a few minutes to himself, watching as Haven approached the mound of brown earth. Phillip found it hard to believe the vibrant animal that Haven had taken on their ride a few days earlier was no more.

The mist turned into light rain. "Haven," he said softly, "we should...." The words died on his lips as he saw Haven's head bow and then his shoulders bobbing up and down. Walking to him, Phillip touched Haven's shoulder and felt Haven's hand cover his. Looking, he saw the tears run down his cheeks.

"He was always my friend, no matter what. Since I was thirteen, I always had him, and he's gone."

Phillip said nothing—there was nothing to say that didn't sound like a ridiculous platitude. Instead, Phillip stood next to Haven as he talked about the things he and Jake had done. As he listened, Phillip began to understand just how important Jake had been to Haven. The rain increased, and Phillip felt it run down his back, plastering his clothes to his skin, but Haven made no move to leave, watching as the water darkened the mound of earth as it soaked into the ground.

Finally Haven turned to him, eyes questioning, as if he just realized they were standing in the rain. "Let's get inside before we wash away out here," Haven told him as he walked back toward the ATV. "Why didn't you say something?"

"Because you needed time with Jake worse than I needed to remain dry." Phillip climbed on behind Haven. "Besides, I won't melt." The engine started, drowning out further speech, but Phillip thought he heard something about being made of sugar.

Back at the house and dry again, Phillip wandered into the living room, letting Haven change in peace while he wiped up the water from the floor. They'd both arrived dripping wet and wandered through the house. Phillip had ushered Haven into the bathroom and gotten him some clothes. Listening, he heard Haven moving in the other room—at least he thought it was Haven; it could have been Jefferson's nurse. "Phillip, I need to go back home."

He looked up and saw Haven standing barefoot near the entrance to the living room, sweatpants hanging on his hips. If the man hadn't been so miserable, Phillip would have tugged him into the bedroom and kissed the frown off his face and a lot more. But now his heart ripped open for the man, and he wanted to protect him. Phillip actually shivered even though it was warm. *Where in hell had that come from?* "Of course you can, anytime. Do you want me to go with you?"

"I don't know what I want. Staying here is nice and safe, but it feels like I'm running away from where I should be. The ranch and Kade, they need me. I can't just up and leave them because I'm hurting." Haven began to shake, and Phillip dropped the towel, hurrying to him, embracing him.

"Actually, you can, for a few days at least," Phillip said, and he heard heavy footsteps coming down the hall.

"Phillip's right. You've been through a lot. Of course you're welcome to go home, but we're all just worried about you," Dakota said.

"I know. It's just...." Haven sighed, and Phillip could tell he was trying to keep himself from falling apart again.

"Then let's go back to your house. That way we can check to make sure everything's okay." Phillip didn't let go, holding tighter. Somehow he had to let Haven know he wasn't alone, and this was the only way he could think of to do that right now.

"Okay," Dakota agreed, leaving the room and returning with jackets. "It's raining cats and dogs out there."

"You're coming too?" Haven asked, still in Phillip's arms, where Phillip wanted him to stay for a long time.

"I figure I can talk with Kade to make sure there isn't anything he needs. We're all here for you, Haven. All you have to do is ask, and that means backing off when you want us to, as well."

Phillip released the hug and slipped on his jacket while Haven and Dakota got theirs on too. Leaving the house, they dodged raindrops as they hurried to Dakota's truck. Slamming the door, Dakota drove to Haven's.

When they arrived, Haven sat looking at the house, making no move to get out. "We don't have to do this now, you know," Dakota said softly, but Haven popped the door. Climbing out, he walked toward the front door, inserting his key and pushing it open.

"Would you like something to drink?" Haven asked as though this was some sort of social call. At first Phillip thought it weird, but he realized Haven was just trying to do normal things. And welcoming guests to your home was normal.

"That'd be great, thank you," Dakota answered, and Haven returned with three open beers, handing one to each of them.

"I don't know what I expected," Haven said, standing in the middle of the living room looking completely lost. "I sort of thought it would feel or look different, but it doesn't. Everything looks the same; it even feels the same. It's just that Dad isn't about to come out of his office and tell me what I did wrong." Haven took a swig of beer, but Phillip wasn't thirsty. "Dad," Haven started to say, "you left me with a mess."

"How so?" Dakota asked. "The place looks kept up and clean. The ranch itself is older but usable. You've got great land and a healthy herd."

"That's because that's all the stuff that I did. Dad took care of the books and the money, so I have no idea if we're making money or if I'm about to lose the ranch because we have too many debts to pay." Haven took another gulp of beer, finishing his off and reaching for the one Phillip had yet to touch.

"Easy, there," Dakota cautioned lightly. "That's not the way to deal with this. Phillip's an accountant. He could probably look at the books for you, if you like, and as far as the ranch goes, we'll help. Hell, half the town will if you ask them."

Haven set down the beer, to Phillip's relief, and started down the hall. "The office is in there. I really don't know where anything is, but you're welcome to look if you want. I don't even know what to look for."

"Why don't you come with me," Phillip said. "That way you'll know what I'm doing."

"I'm going out to check with Kade, see if I can give him a hand. I'll be back inside in a while," Dakota said as he headed outside. Haven led Phillip to a closed door, opening it, and he and Phillip stepped inside. The office was meticulously clean, with a computer, desk, and file cabinets.

"Let's boot up the computer and start there," Phillip commented as he sat in the chair, moving the mouse and breathing a sigh as the computer desktop showed. He'd been worried the whole system might be password protected. He found a simple accounting program and opened it, losing himself in the numbers for a while. "According to this, it looks like the ranch has been making money, good money, for a while." Phillip motioned Haven around and showed him the figures. "Your dad kept good records." Phillip looked up at the filing cabinets and pulled on a drawer marked "Bank Statements," but it wouldn't budge. "They're locked." Phillip tried opening them a few more times. "Why would he lock filing cabinets in his own house?" Haven shrugged, but said nothing. "Can you think where he might have put the keys? We can break into the cabinets, but it'll make a huge mess of them."

Haven opened the top right desk drawer and began fishing around in the back of it. "I wasn't supposed to know where these were, but I saw him putting them away once. Why he wouldn't trust his own son...." Haven pulled out a chain with two small keys on it.

Taking the keys, Phillip inserted first one and then the other before turning the lock and opening the bank statement drawer. Everything was laid out by quarter and year. Phillip searched in the most recent quarter and found last month's bank statements, pulling them out of the envelopes before spreading them on the desk. "This looks like the account he used for payroll." Phillip checked the amounts with the payroll accounting entries to confirm. "And this looks like the general account for the ranch, but according to the records, there should be more money here." Phillip looked over the statements and easily matched payments from the records.

Slightly confused, he looked at another set of statements and whistled. "Here's the money," Phillip said, and he handed Haven the statement.

The younger man whistled as he looked at the balance. "Ninety thousand dollars?"

"Yes, but look at the name on the account." Phillip pointed out. "Your dad put the account in his name. Not the ranch, but his alone." Phillip looked through the statements. "And there are more like that," he said as he handed Haven additional statements. "At least five, and they're all in his name." Looking up from the computer screen as his mind whirled with the implications of what he'd found, Phillip glanced at Haven and his fingers stopped mid-type.

"Was my own father stealing from me?"

"Not necessarily," Phillip went on. "I mean, the ranch was his, so putting the money in his own name could have been his way of separating the ranch and his personal money." He felt himself going into accountant mode, the numbers and figures speaking to him like they always did.

Haven touched his arm, and this time there was no mistaking the pain in Haven's eyes. "But it wasn't his, not alone. When my grandfather died, he left half the ranch to me and half to my father. My part was in trust until I became an adult, so by moving the money into his own name, he was stealing, because at least half of it was mine. Are there any other accounts?" Phillip saw a frantic look appear in Haven's eyes, and he began tearing through the filing cabinet, pulling out bank statements, opening other drawers. "There have to be accounts for me."

Phillip got up from the chair, pulling Haven into his arms. "If there are, we'll find them, I promise." He had to do something for

Haven. *Damn, he shouldn't have done any of this now.* "Would you mind if I packed up some of these records? I'd like to go through them in a lot more detail." No matter what he'd told Haven, what he'd found so far did not look good to him at all. It seemed like Haven's dad was building himself a nest egg at Haven's expense. The thought nearly had Phillip fuming, and if Haven weren't with him, he'd probably be muttering under his breath and calling the man every name in the book.

"No, take whatever you need," Haven said against his shoulder, having stopped shaking. "I want to get out of here."

That sounded like a wonderful idea to Phillip too. Releasing Haven from the hug, Phillip took his hand and led him out of the office. In the hall, Haven tugged him into his bedroom, and Phillip thought for a second....

"I want to show you something," Haven said and began reaching under his mattress. What Haven drew out was the last thing he expected to see: an old photograph. "Years ago, my dad went through things and threw out a lot of stuff. When he wasn't looking, I poked through it and found this." Haven handed him the photograph. "I remember him. That's me on my first pony. His name was Caramel, and that," Haven said, pointing to a woman standing next to him, "is the only picture I have of my mother. She left when I was seven or so. Sometimes I can barely remember her, but I can remember when this picture was taken." He sighed softly.

"Do you miss her?" Phillip asked softly, studying the picture. "You have her eyes," he said, brushing his hand over Haven's cheek. "She's beautiful."

Haven shrugged. "It's hard to miss someone you hardly knew. When I was younger, I did. I remember crying for her when she left, but Dad only got mad if he heard me, so that stopped pretty quickly." Haven set the picture on his dresser. "At least I don't have to hide it anymore."

The door banging closed seemed to pull Haven out of his thoughts. "How are you guys doing?" Dakota's voice boomed through the house.

"Fine," Philip answered before turning back to Haven. "If it's okay, I'd like to come back tomorrow and go through the records." He hated bringing up that subject again, but there was a puzzle here, and part of him needed to figure it out. He also hoped some answers would give Haven a modicum of peace. *Because what kind of father steals from his own son?*

"Sure," Haven answered softly.

"Do you want to stay here or come back with Dakota and me?" Phillip asked.

Haven chewed his lower lip worriedly. "I can't keep imposing on Wally and Dakota." Haven's eyes looked all around the room. Phillip knew how he'd feel in this situation. He'd never lived here, but the house itself felt tainted to him, like it had been poisoned by the person who had lived here.

"You're not imposing," Phillip said and looked into Haven's eyes. "I want you to come back. You don't have to, and I'll understand if you want to stay here. This is your home, and if you're more comfortable here, then that's what's important."

Haven shook his head. "It feels like I've been living with a stranger all my life." Haven left the room, opening the door to the next bedroom, obviously his father's. Phillip peered inside. The room appeared almost sterile, with a bed and dresser, closet door hanging open. There were a few things on the dresser, but the walls were bare, not even a picture of Haven or even one of the horses anywhere. It looked more like an "unwelcome" guest room than a place where someone slept or lived part of their life.

"I see what you mean," Phillip said, stepping inside the room, shivering a little in the warm house. "Let's get out of here. Are there things you need to get?"

Haven shook his head. "If I need something, I can come back." Haven turned and left the room with Phillip following behind, closing the bedroom door, finding Dakota in the living room with Kade sitting next to him on the sofa, both men with their feet on the coffee table.

"Everything's fine, Haven," Kade said, getting up as they came into the room. "Is there anything you need?" Kade engulfed Haven in what appeared to Phillip as a rib-busting hug.

"No, I don't think so. Thanks for taking care of things for me."

"It's not a problem. If it's okay, I'm going to make a final check before heading out. I'll be back first thing in the morning. Have you scheduled your dad's funeral?"

"Yeah. He's being cremated, so the memorial service will be Monday evening with visitation for an hour beforehand," Haven answered. "I didn't want a big to-do over it."

"Well, if you need anything, let me know," Kade said as he turned to leave. "And thanks for the help, Dakota. I appreciate it."

"No problem." Dakota shook Kade's hand as he left. "We should get back too. Are you coming as well?" Dakota asked Haven, and the younger man nodded, putting on his rain jacket before following them out of the house and locking the door.

Phillip stood on the porch for a few seconds, watching as the rain dripped off the roof. Here he was supposedly on vacation and yet he'd helped build animal exercise enclosures and was helping Haven get through the death of his father and his horse. "Holy fuck," he whispered to himself. He should be screaming to go home, but after that morning, going home was the furthest thing from his mind. Wally was absolutely right. He liked Haven, and maybe more than liked him. And after this funeral was over, Phillip intended to discover just what Haven's feelings were toward him.

"You coming?" Dakota called, and Phillip hurried down the steps, dodging raindrops as he rushed to the truck.

At Dakota's, they had dinner, and Phillip noticed that Haven was unusually quiet, even given the last few days. Phillip helped Wally clear the dishes, and Haven joined Dakota after he brought Jefferson out into the living room, the sound of the baseball game carrying through the house.

"How's he doing?" Wally asked as he stacked dishes in the dishwasher.

"As well as can be expected, I guess." Phillip told Wally what he'd found at Haven's. "I'm not sure what's going on, but I have a suspicion Haven's dad was trying to put something over on him. He and I are going to go back over there tomorrow, and I'm going to see if I can unravel this little mystery."

The phone ringing near his ear made Phillip jump, and Wally chuckled as he answered it. "Come on in and sit down," Dakota called from the other room. Phillip decided to take his advice and joined the guys, sitting next to Haven. Wally hung up the phone, coming into the room a few minutes later.

"Well, that's sweet, I guess," Wally said as he walked to the front of the couch, about to sit next to Haven when Dakota jumped out of his chair, doing his caveman routine, pulling Wally into his arms and onto his lap.

"There, that's better. At least you'll have to sit for at least five minutes now," Dakota said softly. "So what's this news?"

"Kahn will be arriving tomorrow, and they wanted to know if we could take Sheba as well. It seems they acquired them a few years ago, and neither is working out. They're beautiful animals, but none of the trainers will have anything to do with either of them."

"Won't you need another enclosure?"

"I have the three, and that will fill us up for now, but it does mean I need to get the exercise area finished. It shouldn't take much longer if we can get some dry weather. We just need to lay the fencing over the frames."

Dakota hugged Wally closer. "I know you want to care for them, but won't they be dangerous? These aren't old animals like Schian. They're younger and more energetic."

"I'm hoping they won't be permanent like Schian. I'm thinking I can probably take care of any health issues and then start calling zoos to see if they can take them. They are endangered, after all, and I suspect the circus came by them in a less-than-proper way, probably from across the border," Wally explained as his fingers worked open a button on Dakota's shirt, a hand sliding inside.

Phillip tore his eyes away from the lovebirds, looking to Haven, who slipped a hand around his back, tugging him close as he yawned. "I'm glad I'm exciting," Phillip quipped, knowing Haven had to be completely exhausted.

Haven rolled his eyes before getting up. "Good night," he said to the room, and Phillip noticed for the first time that Jefferson was already asleep in his chair. Wally scooted off Dakota's lap, and the big cowboy wheeled his father down to his room to put him to bed.

"I'll see you in the morning," Wally said before following Dakota out of the room. "Just turn out the lights when you go to bed."

Phillip said he would. Grabbing the remote, he turned off the television, curling onto the sofa, listening to the sounds in the house. He'd always lived alone, and except for vacations and stuff and, of course, college, he hadn't lived with anyone for any length of time. Listening to the sounds in the house, the soft chuckles, water running, footsteps in the hall, the closing of doors and "good night" wishes drifting in the air, Phillip began to realize just what he'd been missing.

"Are you coming to bed?" Haven leaned over the back of the sofa, half-dressed and close enough that Phillip could smell the soap he'd used to clean up.

"I think I better sleep here tonight." *For your own good.* Phillip found he was becoming attached to the man, very attached, and he was also coming to realize just how much he desired him. If he stayed with Haven in the same bed, he really didn't think he could keep his hands off, and after the days Haven had had, the last thing the man needed was to be mauled.

Haven didn't say anything, wandering back down the hall, looking back at him with a kicked-puppy look before disappearing into the bedroom. Phillip squeezed his eyes closed, trying to figure out what to do, when he found himself on his feet and outside the bedroom door. Pushing the door open, he saw Haven sitting on the edge of the bed.

"What did I do?"

*Fuck and damn.* That wasn't what Phillip had meant. Stepping into the room, Phillip closed the door. "You didn't do anything," Phillip said softly, sitting on the bed next to Haven, "other than smell like desire, and every time I get near you I want you, like I wanted you when we were sleeping under the stars. But this isn't the right time for that, and I'm afraid that if I spend another night holding you close with your skin next to mine...."

Haven said nothing, but turned his head, kissing the words away. "I want you, Phillip," Haven whispered softly, pressing him back onto the mattress. "I want to forget for a while. I need to forget everything for a while."

"Are you sure?"

Haven nodded, eyes blazing with hope. "I don't know if I can, but I need to let go of things, and I don't know how. Can you show me?"

Phillip got up, turning off the overhead light, leaving a small light burning in one corner. "Take off your clothes and lie on your back in the middle of the bed." Phillip watched as Haven's T-shirt lifted and slipped off his body. Phillip unbuttoned his own shirt, watching every move Haven made as those gray sweatpants slid down his legs. Damn, that butt was beautiful, and he wanted a taste of that skin. *No, this is about him, not you.* Phillip draped his shirt over a chair, toeing off his shoes before opening his belt and slipping off his pants. They'd already been together, but it had been so dark, and this was the first time either of them would actually see the other naked. "Head back on the pillow, arms by your side," Phillip instructed lightly, "breathe deeply, and let it all out. Relax and just breathe. Don't think about anything other than the sound of my voice." Phillip tried to remain calm and level, but the sight of Haven naked on the bed nearly became his undoing. The man was freakin' gorgeous. Muscles and a body built by a lifetime of hard work—lean, strong, powerful all over.

Climbing on the bed, Phillip straddled Haven's lower legs, running his hands over Haven's knees and powerful quads. "Don't lift your head to look at me. Settle back on the pillow, close your eyes, and breathe." Phillip wished he had some massage oil, but made do with a bit of hand lotion he had on the dresser. "That's it." He kept soothing. "Think of nothing but my hands on your skin." Phillip massaged up Haven's legs, running his hands near his inner thigh and along his hip, tracing the inner pelvic lines.

Haven's breath caught, and then he began breathing again. "That feels really good."

"That's how it's supposed to feel, good and warm enough to make everything else go away." Phillip kept moving his hands, making long ovals over his lover's stomach and back down to his hips, fingers just missing his cock. Haven growled deeply a few times, but Phillip let that go and kept stroking. Elongating the ovals, his fingers passed over Haven's nipples, sliding the buds between two fingers before his hands slipped away again. Over and over, Phillip massaged and stroked. Haven's arousal increased, and Phillip felt the tension slip from his lover's body. "Roll over, Haven," Phillip instructed, and Haven turned beneath him. "Now, there are a few rules."

"Okay," Haven answered softly.

"You are not to move your hips unless I give you permission, and you have to tell me right away if I do something you don't like. Okay?"

"Yes, Phillip," Haven said, and Phillip squirted some lotion on his hands, massaging the skin of Haven's wide back. "That's nice," Haven moaned softly as Phillip worked his way down, fingers doing their best to work away all the tension. Squirting a little more lotion, Phillip worked lower, hands moving over Haven's cheeks, fingers kneading the hard globes. "Phillip." Haven's voice sounded tentative, but he didn't stop him, so Phillip slipped the side of his hand between Haven's cheeks, fingers working one globe hard, the skin and muscle getting worked by his hands.

Sliding his hands away, Phillip gave the other cheek the same treatment, fingers working Haven's butt until the man moaned outright. This time Phillip didn't stop with massage. When he moved his hands away, he trailed his fingers down Haven's crease, skimming lightly over his opening. "Did you like that?"

"Yes," Haven mumbled, neck and back arching.

"Lie back down and don't do that again, or I'll stop." Phillip pulled his hands away, and Haven rested back on the mattress. Spreading Haven's cheeks, Phillip worked his fingers down Haven's crease, fluttering them over his opening before moving them away again. Leaning forward, Phillip placed his lips against Haven's skin, licking and sucking as he tasted the salty sweetness. Damn, this man was sweet, and Phillip slid his tongue along Haven's cleft, zeroing in on his opening.

"Phillip, what are you doing?" Haven asked, voice trembling, but to his credit, he didn't move.

"Do you like it?" Phillip asked, blowing his breath over the wet skin. Haven nodded his answer. "Then remember the rules," Phillip reminded him as he returned to what he was doing, pointing his tongue, loosening still more of Haven's muscles.

"I will, but you're making my head all spinny."

"That's good," Phillip said as he got his fingers into the act, sliding them over the smooth skin. Licking one, Phillip worked the wet finger around Haven's opening, teasing the skin before working it inside. Haven hissed but then got quiet as though he were holding his breath, waiting to see what would happen next. "Breathe, honey, deep and thorough," Phillip soothed as he slipped his finger away. Spreading Haven's legs wide, Phillip continued working those muscles, fully tasting his lover to a litany of small moans and whimpers. Working his hand beneath Haven, he lifted his hips slightly, stroking Haven's cock as he worked his butt.

"Phillip, can I?"

"Yes," he answered, and Haven began thrusting into his hand as Phillip worked his tongue deep into Haven's searing heat.

"I'm gonna, Phillip!" Haven cried out hoarsely as he coated Phillip's hand and fingers with his release. Phillip slipped his hand away from Haven's skin, picking up a T-shirt from the floor, wiping his hand, and after rolling Haven over, he wiped his lover's skin before getting out of the bed and turning off the light. "What about you?" Haven asked even as he snuggled close.

"It's okay, just go to sleep." Phillip released his breath, his body on overdrive with every one of Haven's touches, but soon he heard Haven's breathing even out and knew the younger man was asleep. If Haven got some relief from his grief and worries, a little frustration was more than worth it.

*Chapter Nine*

HAVEN woke up, staring at the ceiling in his room, the same room he'd slept in for as long as he could remember. Except he couldn't sleep; his mind wouldn't let him, and that mark on the ceiling wasn't going to move or change no matter how long he looked at it. Getting up, he pulled on a pair of sweats and wandered through the house, eventually pushing open the door to his dad's office. Sitting at the desk in the dark room, he turned on the computer and stared at the screen, hoping for some sort of inspiration to make everything clear. Nothing came.

Before the funeral, he and Phillip had had every intention of going through his father's records with a fine-toothed comb, but fate, neighbors, and old friends had other ideas. No sooner had they booted up the PC than a knock on the door announced that the ladies from the church had arrived, ushering in a buffet of food and a steady stream of people stopping by to pay their respects and to tell him how much they cared for his father. It was nice to know his dad was liked and to listen to people tell their stories about him. But try as he might, Haven could not get past the thought that his dad might have been stealing from him. It was almost as though the idea had tainted his memories.

Yesterday had been a complete blur, with the memorial service and still more people stopping by or wanting to talk to him before and after the service. The hardest thing was that he'd invited anyone who wished to say a few words, and the one thing that had warmed his heart was the number of people who'd stood up and told stories about his dad. He knew his dad wasn't a saint, but he'd smiled when old friends talked about his dad's football days and what he was like when he was younger. Those stories and the genuine caring of old friends made the doubts and worry recede at least for a while, but now, there it was, playing over and over again. He desperately wanted answers, and even more, wanted to know that his father was still the man who'd bought him his first pony.

After the funeral, he'd insisted on coming back to the house. It was time, and he couldn't hide from his life and responsibilities anymore. But now, in the middle of the night, sitting alone in his dad's office, he regretted that decision more than he could possibly say. Throughout everything, Phillip had been there for him. Staying nearby and talking to all the ladies who visited before the funeral when the last thing Haven wanted to do was talk, and he was there at night, taking care of him, making things stop so he could sleep, at least for a while. He knew that he needed to get used to being alone. Because that was what he was. Not that he felt that way when Phillip was around, but Haven knew he'd be stupid to think Phillip would stay forever. He wouldn't. Eventually, he'd go back home and return to his life, leaving Haven here to take care of his ranch. Hence the need to go home and the reason he sat alone in an office in the middle of the night instead of in a bed with Phillip holding him all night. "You can't get used to it, because Phillip won't always be there," he admonished himself out loud, lowering his head to the top of the desk. Haven thought of going through more of the files to see if he could find something, but even if he found the answer, he probably wouldn't recognize it, anyway.

Getting up, Haven left the room, wandering into the living room and flopping onto the sofa. Haven turned on the television, curling himself in a blanket as the images on the screen cast flickering shadows on the walls. Haven must have fallen asleep, although for the life of him he couldn't remember it, because he opened his eyes and saw Phillip leaning over the back of the sofa looking down at him. "You're so cute when you sleep," Phillip whispered. "Your nose crinkles just a little sometimes, like you're dreaming you're a bunny or something."

"How long have you been here?" Haven asked, not sure if he should be offended by the "cute" remark or not.

"A while. Everyone's up and about." He tilted his head. "Kahn decided to caterwaul for most of the night. Poor thing's having trouble adjusting to his new home. At least that's what Wally says." Phillip's eyes glinted with mischief. "Dakota said if he does it again tonight, they'll have a beautiful tiger skin rug in front of the fireplace."

Haven pushed back the blanket and sat up. "I bet that went over well." Haven inhaled deeply and smelled coffee.

"He wasn't serious, and Wally knew it." Phillip backed away, his head disappearing. "I made coffee."

"Thank you," Haven said as he wandered into the kitchen, retrieving two mugs from the cupboard before pouring and handing one to Phillip with a yawn. "I didn't sleep all night," Haven admitted, yawning again.

"Neither did I," Phillip admitted, and Haven found himself incredibly pleased. "It seems that I sleep much better with a certain heat generator in the same bed with me."

"Heat generator?" Haven asked with a lift of his eyebrows, and he saw Phillip step closer, setting his mug on the counter. Haven did the same, managing to get his mug settled before Phillip's lips met his, and Haven could no longer think of anything but the way those lips felt against his. Memories of the last couple of nights when Phillip had "relaxed" him had his heart racing and his body anything but relaxed.

"Yes," Phillip said against his lips, "you generate more heat than any man I've ever met." Haven felt Phillip's erection grinding into his hip as his own reacted. "I missed you last night and this morning," Phillip whispered against his lips, hot breath tickling his skin before he kissed Haven again, lips moving against his, tongue devouring his mouth, palm cradling his head, deepening the kiss still further.

Phillip moved backward, lugging him along, and the next thing he knew they tumbled onto the sofa, all arms and legs. Haven felt his sweatpants slide down, fingers grasping his cock firmly, tugging. He tried to moan, but Phillip kissed it away. Haven tried to get Phillip out of his clothes, but every time he reached for him, Phillip tugged a little more, or wrapped his lips around one of his nipples, kissing and teasing his thoughts away.

Another hand joined the first, fingers slipping between his legs, teasing his opening. He saw Phillip bring his fingers to his mouth, licking them before sliding them back between his legs, and slowly he felt Phillip's finger breach his body while Phillip's other hand gripped his cock even tighter. At first he tried to slide away, not sure he liked the sensations, but then Phillip touched something, and stars and lights shot behind his eyes. "I knew you'd like that," Phillip said knowingly, kissing him again before shifting, tongue sliding around his crown, the finger going deeper.

Haven bucked, Phillip's mouth taking him deeper, the finger sliding away. When he relaxed, Phillip's mouth slipped away and the finger slid deep, touching that spot. Haven clamped down, his eyes closed, hips bucking, brain working feverishly on how to get both sensations at once, the teasing frustration driving his desire higher. Moving faster, Haven bucked harder, driving his cock deep into Phillip's talented mouth. "I need more, please," Haven moaned, but Phillip remained steadfast as Haven's climax stayed just out of reach.

Phillip slipped his lips away. "I want you to come for me, just like this. Wanna taste you."

"I can't," Haven whined softly, cutting off when Phillip took him again.

"Yes, you can. Do it for me." Phillip didn't say anything, but Haven felt his frustration and desire drive him further, higher, the precipice just out of reach until something clicked deep inside. Yes, he could, and he would. Bucking forward, he felt his mind take over, driving him further until he could barely think at all before soaring over the top as he climaxed hard, pouring himself into Phillip.

Haven felt his head bonk back against the arm of the sofa, his body completely wrung out. Taking a second to catch his breath, he looked to Phillip and saw him smiling back. Squirming out from under Phillip, Haven knelt on the sofa, reaching for Phillip, kissing him hard as he finally managed to get the man's pants open and his shirt undone. Shifting to his belly, Haven arched his back and took Phillip's heavy shaft as deep as he could, tongue sliding along the underside. Phillip groaned, a deep, rich sound, as Haven sucked. "God, Haven," Phillip moaned softly as Haven saw his lover's back arch and flex and his hips begin to move. "You're getting damn good at this." Haven didn't answer, but the praise and Phillip's obvious enjoyment spurred him on, and he threw himself into pleasing Phillip, listening for those moans. Fingers carded through his hair, and Phillip began to thrust. "Haven," Phillip said softly, and he sucked harder, feeling Phillip stiffen further, and then his lover was coming, full and hard.

Slipping from his mouth, Phillip shifted, joining him on the sofa, caressing his skin as he pulled him close. "Was I okay?" Haven asked.

Phillip shook his head slowly, swallowing. "You were amazing. Completely amazing." With Phillip's words in his ears, Haven closed his eyes. Opening them again, he hadn't realized he'd fallen asleep, but he must have, because Phillip had as well, his soft snoring an audible testament. Haven's stirring woke the other man, and Phillip smiled at him before lifting his head to look around. "Good God," he said when he saw the state of their clothes. Haven was nearly naked, but Phillip's clothes hung at all kinds of strange angles, with his pants bunched around his knees. "I guess you wore me out."

"I'm just grateful Kade didn't decide to come inside, or we'd probably scare the man away for good," Haven said. They both laughed while Phillip pulled his clothes back on.

"As much as I'd love to spend the day in bed with you, or on the couch with you, or anywhere naked with you, I came over to see if I could help out with those accounts."

Haven sat up, pulling on his sweats. "I know. It was just kind of nice to forget them for a while."

"Yeah, but maybe we'll find something that explains everything."

Haven wasn't holding out much hope of that, but he nodded and showed Phillip to the office before continuing on to the bathroom.

Showered and dressed, he peered into the office, seeing Phillip hard at work typing away at the computer and making notes on a pad of paper. Stepping back, he continued through the house and out into the morning sunshine.

"Hey, sleepyhead," Kade called as he carried a load of soiled bedding from the barn, "I was starting to think you were going to sleep all day."

"No, just half of it," Haven called back. "Phillip is in the office looking through the accounts. I don't know how long he'll be, but I need to check on the herds."

Kade nodded. "And there's a section of paddock fence that needs mending once I'm done here." Kade set down the handles of the wheelbarrow. "I was wondering what you'd like me to do with Jake's gear."

"Just set it aside for now. I'm hoping that after everything's settled I can afford to get another horse." He hated the thought of replacing Jake, but they'd need another animal for work. He needed to get over the loss first, though.

"I'll take care of it," Kade said, but instead of moving away, he continued looking at him like he had more to say.

"What is it?"

"Well," Kade said, slipping off his glove and running his hand across the back of his neck, "I've been kind of thinking about leaving. I don't mean quitting so much as moving away. My mom's sister and her husband have a ranch near Montana, and they asked me to come work for them. They need someone to help manage the herds, and they'd eventually like me to take over the whole operation. They don't have any kids of their own, and they'd like the ranch to remain in the family, so...." Kade squirmed a little, and Haven wasn't quite sure how to react. "I told them I couldn't leave for a few months, but they'd like me to come for a visit in a few weeks to work out the details. You aren't mad, are you?"

A myriad of emotions raced through him, running the gambit from happiness for his friend to fear about what he was going to do without him. "Of course I'm not mad. I'm happy for you. It's a great opportunity, one you certainly can't pass up." Haven did his best to smile—it seemed like everyone was leaving. "Will you be back?"

"Of course, and we'll see each other at the wedding," Kade said with mock seriousness before bursting into a grin. "I was hoping you'd be my best man."

Haven broke into a huge grin. "Of course I will."

"Good. The wedding will be in the church in town next spring. Penny's family is still here, so we'll be back often. You won't be getting rid of me that easily." Kade grinned, his body vibrating with excitement.

"After work, stop by the house and we'll celebrate," Haven said, and Kade agreed, picking up the wheelbarrow and going back to work with a spring in his step.

Haven walked back toward the house, listening for the click of computer keys. "Phillip, I'll be checking the herds. If you need me, call my cell."

"Okay," he heard from the office, and Haven went back to the barn. His first impulse was to go to Jake's stall, and he had to stop himself. Saddling his father's horse, Dusty, Haven set off across the range toward the east where the bulk of the herd was grazing. Unlike with Jake, who he had always talked to as he rode, Haven was quiet and contemplative, thinking about Phillip, his father, the ranch. Working outside on the range always calmed him, but today that grounded feeling he usually got seemed missing. He wasn't grounded, not any longer. His dad was gone and might have been.... "Fuck...," he said out loud. He did not want to think about that for the millionth time. "Phillip is inside trying to figure out what he can, and you have to let him." Whatever his dad had been doing, Haven couldn't change it. All he could do was figure it out and correct what he could.

The land seemed quiet and for that Haven was grateful. As he approached the herd, he stayed far enough away so as not to spook them, but close enough that he could get a good look. Everything seemed fine. Walking the perimeter, Haven looked for wolf tracks and other signs of predators, but saw nothing. The beasties seemed content to munch on their grass.

As the sun peaked overhead, Haven headed back toward the ranch house. Settling Dusty in one of the paddocks, Haven walked into the house, and was surprised to see Phillip reclining on the sofa with a beer in hand. "I take it you found something," Haven said, not sure if he should be relieved or worried.

"I did, and I'm not sure how you're going to feel about it," Phillip replied. "Why don't you get yourself a beer, and I'll tell you what I think."

Haven did just that, opening the refrigerator door and grabbing a beer along with a leftover meat and cheese tray, carrying them both back with him. "So," Haven said as he flopped down on the sofa, "what is it he was doing?"

"I think your dad was getting ready to sell the ranch," Phillip said levelly and then seemed to brace himself.

"He what? His grandparents started this place, decades ago. Why would he do that? You must be wrong," Haven professed, even as doubt crept in.

Phillip shook his head slowly. "I don't think so. He was stockpiling cash, as you saw in those accounts, and he seemed to be liquidating. Over the past few years, he stopped purchasing anything that he didn't need. You must know that?" Haven did. He'd practically had to beg his dad to spend money on anything. "He also had parts of the land surveyed. Mind you, I don't have a smoking gun like a real estate listing, but I'm pretty sure that was what he had in mind."

"But he couldn't sell, not without my permission," Haven explained. "I own part of the ranch."

"In trust," Phillip said, "and I found those papers as well. It seems he still had power of attorney until you exercised your rights, so as long as he said nothing and you didn't revoke it, he could indeed sell the property or at least by the time you realized what was going on, it could have been too late." Phillip leaned forward, rolling some of the lunchmeat around a square of cheese. "I found at least half a million dollars in accounts, and I was able to match deposits into those accounts with withdrawals from either ranch accounts or deductions from payments received."

"Why would he do this?" Haven felt as though he were going to be sick.

"I don't know your dad. I only met him the one time, but I think he probably thought of the ranch as his, and that all the money it made was his as well."

"Goddamn him!" Haven yelled at the ceiling, doing his best to breathe and keep from punching the wall. "Why did he have to be such a completely selfish bastard?"

He sank back onto the sofa, letting his mind ponder over Phillip's idea. In his heart he knew, no matter how much he might wish to deny it, what Phillip said was probably true. It made sense—the cutting back on expenses, the reluctance to replace anything, his near total lack of interest in anything around the ranch except the books and his accounts. "How long had he been planning this?"

"The surveys were done a little over a year ago," Phillip answered, and Haven saw him leaning forward, watching him intently. "I'm sorry, Haven, but it looks like he'd been planning this for a while. The lying bastard." Phillip got up, and Haven watched as he started pacing the room. "Look, I think you better get a lawyer." Phillip continued walking back and forth.

Haven wanted to join him. Punching the sofa cushion, Haven wanted to scream, but knew that wouldn't do any good. The man was dead, and he had to somehow pick up the pieces. "Wait, why do I need a lawyer?"

"To make sure his will is probated properly. I found a copy in the office. At least he had the decency to leave everything to you, but you need to make sure everything is handled correctly so you don't have issues down the road." Phillip finally stopped pacing, standing in front of him. "How can you be so calm about this? I'm mad as hell, and he didn't do this to me."

Haven knew he should be angry, but he was too hurt right now. "My father died, and afterwards I find out he was a complete fucktard bastard. I knew he didn't really love me. Don't know why, I was his son, but he never really did." Haven sighed. He was so tired, physically, emotionally. "I guess I should be mad, but I don't have the time or the energy. I have to pick up the pieces and figure out what I'm going to do. I still have the ranch, and I have the money Dad socked away." Haven looked to Phillip. "Do you think you were able to find it all?"

Phillip's eyes lit up. "Yeah. It took some time, but I was able to figure out the intervals and the ways he transferred the money. He was meticulous in his records, that was for sure, and even though he was socking money away like a squirrel, he kept detailed records of every transaction. He had accounts in what looks like every bank in the county. He also had money in some online banks. I was able to find the online statements, but I don't have the passwords to access the accounts. That's something the lawyer should be able to help you with as well." Phillip sat down. "What are you going to do?"

"What I've always done, I guess." Haven rested his head on Phillip's shoulder. "Keep the ranch going somehow. It's not as though I won't have the money, but it just got harder. Kade's leaving too," Haven said, as everything slammed into him at once—his dad, Jake, Kade moving away. Closing his eyes, Haven felt like yelling and crying all at the same time. His life hadn't been perfect, but it had been familiar and relatively safe and happy. Now it was a complete mess, and everything seemed to be falling around his ankles. "I need time to think," Haven said softly, almost to himself.

"Do you want me to go?" Phillip asked.

"No. Yes." Haven sighed. "Fuck, I don't know." He lifted his head. "You'll leave eventually, just like everyone else." Haven straightened up, sitting back. "This is just a vacation for you and some fun with the ranch kid. In a week or two, you'll go home and leave just like everyone else." Haven felt his voice rise over the jumbled thoughts and feelings in his head. "So maybe you should just go now too. It'll save me the added pain of saying goodbye to someone else I thought cared for me." His emotions skating close to the surface, Haven jumped to his feet, turning away so he could do this.

"Haven," Phillip said softly, hurt plain in his voice, and Haven nearly relented, his heart practically begged him to. Fuck, it had already happened. He'd fallen in love with Phillip like some stupid lovesick teenager falling for the first person who showed him any kindness. He'd known Phillip's being here was only temporary, and yet he'd gone and fallen in love anyway.

"Phillip." Haven's voice nearly broke, and he only held himself together through sheer force of will. "It was fun, but I think I need to figure out what I'm going to do here, and you need to go back to your vacation. I just can't do this. I'm sorry. I can't play with my heart like this—it's just too fragile right now." Haven could almost see Phillip reaching out from behind him, and he stepped away.

"Haven, I'm not leaving right away, and I thought…."

He waved Phillip silent. "I can't, Phillip. Don't you see that? I have a life and a ranch to try to rebuild and…." Haven's emotions broke through the last bit of control holding him together. "I fell in love with you, Phillip, and if I have any hope of keeping my heart intact, I just can't keep this up anymore. I can't deny how I feel, and I know I won't be able to bear you leaving in a few weeks. Yes, we can be together and have fun, but I'll spend the entire time hoping and wishing that you'd somehow decide to stay, only to have you leave anyway." Haven stared at Phillip, but when he didn't move, Haven did. "If you're not going to leave, I will. There are things I have to take care of in town." Haven forced his feet to move toward the door, hoping like hell Phillip would stop him, listening for Phillip's voice to tell him he loved him too. With every step he took, Haven kept hoping, until the front door closed behind him.

He managed to make it to his truck and out onto the road before his eyes began to blur. Pulling off, he rested his head against the steering wheel and gave in to the grief that had been threatening for days to completely engulf him. Other vehicles passed, but Haven paid no attention, too lost in his own feelings to care. Reaching to the glove compartment, he found a napkin he'd stuffed in there at some point in the distant past, using it to wipe his eyes. Swallowing hard, he pulled back on the road, driving to town over familiar roads, in a bit of a daze.

After getting the supplies that the ranch needed as well as stopping at the store, Haven made a phone call to a lawyer Dakota had recommended. At least the lawyer had listened to him and said he'd look into things. The man actually seemed shocked, which Haven took as a good sign. Haven got back into the truck and left town, heading out to the ranch. Rolling down the windows for fresh air, Haven turned up the radio to drown out his thoughts and soon found himself humming along to the music. Stopping at the corner, Haven signaled for the turn.

"Hey, faggot!" Haven looked toward the source of the sound and saw Herbie's crooked-nosed face hanging out his truck window. "Yeah, you! So what's it like to take it up the ass?"

Before Haven knew what was happening, all his frustrations boiled to the surface, and like a bull, he saw red. Leaping out of the truck, he raced over to Herbie, yanking his door open. "You talking to me, you freaky-faced little shit?" Pulling him out of the truck, Haven was about to land his first punch when he heard the thud of feet on the pavement as Herbie's two friends jumped down from the truck bed.

Herbie sneered as he wrenched out of Haven's grip. "We'll see who's shit when we're done with you, faggot!" Haven never saw the punch to his kidney coming.

*Chapter Ten*

PHILLIP numbly left Haven's house and drove back to Wally and Dakota's. He'd desperately hoped to find Wally around, but his truck wasn't parked in the yard, and Phillip figured he was out on a call. Walking inside, he did find Jefferson in the living room asleep in his chair, with golf on the television. Phillip went into the room, sitting on the sofa, watching, but not paying attention to the television.

"Kid," he heard Jefferson say softly, "what's got you looking like a kicked dog?" As if on cue, one of Wally and Dakota's mutts nosed open the door, wandering indoors before jumping on the sofa. The big black mutt climbed over the arm of the sofa, hind legs on the arm, front legs on Jefferson's chair so he could put his head on the man's lap as Jefferson rested his curled hand on the dog's back. "Boy trouble?"

"I guess you could say that," Phillip said, without looking away from the television.

"Things have changed, haven't they, son?" Jefferson said remarkably clearly. "The old ways aren't working."

"No, but I'm not sure I want them to." Phillip turned on the sofa. "Are you sure you want to hear this?"

Jefferson smiled the half smile that Phillip had come to read as the equivalent of a grin from anyone else. "Sure, let me have it. After listening to Wally and Dakota sometimes, there ain't nothing anybody can do to shock me. It's amazing what folks will do and say when they think you're asleep."

"Jefferson," Phillip said, grinning, "you old dog."

The man sure seemed pleased with himself. "So what's the problem? I may be in a chair, but I still got my brains, though sometimes I think they're a little scrambled." Jefferson moved his permanent fist across the dog's back.

"Haven," Phillip said. "No, that's not right. Haven's not the problem, I am," Phillip corrected. "See, I…." *God, this was hard.*

"You go from man to man having a good time, like one of the bulls, but never staying around for very long," Jefferson said in his colorful way.

"Yeah, the thing is that I'm not sure if that's what I want with Haven. I know him going back with me isn't really an option. His life is here, and it's all he knows. Besides, he loves this life. I know that." *How could he explain that he just didn't fit in here?*

"And you think you either won't—or don't want to—fit," Jefferson supplied as the dog scooted closer, head slipping under Jefferson's hand for more attention. "Now I'll admit we have a good life here, but it isn't for everyone. It can be harsh and unforgiving at times, but it's also beautiful and wondrous." Phillip saw Jefferson's head shift from the television to the window. "Tell me they got a view like that in Wisconsin." Jefferson kept his gaze on the window, the television clicking off. "Let me ask you this, have you talked to Dakota and Wally about staying?"

"No. I never gave it any thought before," he answered honestly. "Why?" Phillip moved closer, his nose smelling gossip. "What do you know?"

"I may hear plenty, but that don't mean I have a big mouth," Jefferson replied his eyes twinkling. *Damn, the man did know something.* "I'll tell you the same thing I told Dakota last year. You don't get many chances at love, so you gotta go after it and hold on when you find it." Jefferson began breathing heavier, like he was getting tired. "Do you love him? And more to the point, do you think he loves you?"

Phillip thought for a second. "Fuck!" he gasped as what Haven had said kicked in. He'd completely missed it. Haven had said he loved him.

"What?" Jefferson said, his head rolling against the head rests.

Phillip jumped up from the sofa. "I gotta go. I was a complete and utter moron, and I gotta fix it if I can." Phillip hit the front door at a run, banging it back against the stops as he took another step and sailed over the front porch steps, his feet barely touching the ground.

"What's got into you?" David asked as he wiped his hands on a rag near the tap. Phillip's response was a wave as he looked for one of the ranch trucks. He thought of taking his car, but knew the roads would probably shake it apart.

"I need to get to town," Phillip cried to David, who tossed him a set of keys.

"The truck's next to Mario's."

"Thanks," Phillip called as he rushed over, climbing into the cab and starting the engine. As he drove up the drive, Phillip saw Haven's truck turn in, weaving before veering off the driveway and stopping in the middle of Dakota's front yard, such as it was. Phillip stepped on the brake, stopping the truck. He saw the front door of Haven's truck open and a leg emerge. The foot touched the ground, and a second later, Haven toppled out of the truck, landing on the ground in a heap. Phillip threw the truck into park. Without thinking, he scrambled out, racing to Haven.

"Call the ambulance," Phillip shouted and saw David take off for the house, with Mario rushing across the yard toward them. "Call Dakota and Wally! He needs help!" Phillip shouted, before looking at a still Haven, shirt covered in blood. Haven coughed and blood spurted from his mouth. Haven seemed to be breathing, but Phillip wasn't sure if his lungs were filling with blood or not.

"The ambulance is on its way," David told him. "Do you know what happened?"

"From the knuckle marks on his face, I'd say he was beaten," Mario answered, covering Haven with a blanket.

"Don't move," Phillip cautioned Haven, when he felt him trying to get up. "Help is on the way." Jesus, Phillip could feel his heart pounding in his chest. "Where is that fucking ambulance?"

Finally, after what seemed like a year and a day to Phillip, sirens were heard in the distance, getting louder. A truck pulled into the drive, and Phillip saw Dakota get out, the door slamming so hard the entire vehicle shook. David moved his truck out of the middle of the drive as the ambulance, a fire truck, and a police cruiser all pulled into the driveway.

The EMTs hurried out of the ambulance and made their way over, looking Haven over and asking questions that no one could answer. Police officers and firemen asked more questions, but all they could do was provide basic information about who Haven was. "He pulled up in the truck," Phillip said as he pointed to where the truck still stood in the middle of the yard, "and basically fell out. It looks as though he's been beaten up, but I can't tell you by who or exactly what happened." Phillip answered the police officer's questions, chewing his lip as he watched the medical people work on Haven.

"Is he going to be okay?" Phillip asked, not really expecting an answer, but he had to say something.

"I don't know, sir," the police officer said as Phillip continued to watch the EMTs working on Haven. One of them brought a board from the truck, and they maneuvered Haven onto it.

"Where are they taking him?" Phillip asked, looking alternately at the police officer and Dakota, hoping one of them would know.

"They're transporting him to Teton Memorial," the officer answered clinically.

Phillip shook his head. "You're just a fountain of useful information, aren't you?" Phillip glared at the police officer. "Why are you still here? There's obviously nothing you can do for anyone."

"Phillip," Dakota said from next to him, "calm down. It's going to be okay."

"Then have him do something. Haven's hurt bad, and all he's doing is asking stupid questions again and again when he should be out looking for whoever did this to Haven." Phillip felt his control slipping and watched as the EMTs lifted Haven off the ground, carrying him toward the ambulance. Walking over, Phillip looked at Haven as they loaded him into the ambulance, his eyes closed, unmoving. Phillip couldn't even tell if he was breathing. "Can I ride with him?"

"Are you family?" one of the EMTs asked.

"No. His father died a few days ago, and there's no other family in the area. I'm his friend." Phillip nearly bit his lip to keep from telling them he was Haven's boyfriend. After their earlier conversation, he wasn't sure what they were, but damn it, he didn't want to lose Haven.

"There isn't a lot of room," the other EMT said as he climbed into the ambulance.

"We'll follow you," Dakota offered, and he led Phillip to his truck. The fire engine had already left, and the police car followed. Dakota started the engine, and as the ambulance pulled out, Dakota was right behind.

The ambulance seemed to fly, and Dakota drove as fast as he dared, arriving at the hospital a few minutes behind. Dakota dropped Phillip at the emergency entrance, and Phillip explained who he was to the lady at the desk and that he was there because of Haven Jessup. "They just brought him in. The doctors have to do an evaluation first. I'll note on the chart that you're here. You can have a seat in the waiting area."

Not knowing what else to do, Phillip sat. Dakota came in, and after Phillip explained what he'd been told, Dakota sat next to him. "What happened today?" Dakota asked. "I expected you to be with Haven all day."

Phillip explained about what happened as best he could. "The thing is, in a roundabout way, Haven told me he loved me and I missed it." Phillip turned to look at the doors as they opened. "What if I never get the chance to tell him how I feel?"

"What is it you feel?" Dakota asked softly.

Phillip had asked himself that same question ever since he'd left Haven's a few hours earlier. "I'm not really sure. I mean, I've sort of never felt like this before with anyone."

"What does your heart say?" Dakota prompted.

"That I was a fool for not going after Haven earlier and that now I could regret it for the rest of my life." Phillip dabbed his eyes, trying not to carry on like an overworked drama queen. "What should I tell him if I get the chance?"

Dakota smiled, nudging Phillip with his shoulder. "Just be honest, speak from the heart, and everything will be fine. Just be honest with yourself and with him." The door opened, and a man who looked like a doctor walked in their direction.

"Phillip Reardon?" the doctor asked, and Phillip jumped to his feet.

"How's Haven? Is he going to be okay?" The questions tumbled out fast.

"We don't know. He's being prepped for emergency surgery. We believe he has internal injuries. We'll know more in a few hours," the doctor said levelly before turning to leave. Phillip thanked him and then slumped in his chair.

The minutes dragged into what felt like hours. Eventually Wally came rushing in, and after being brought up to date, sat down with them. It was Wally who called Kade and told him what was going on. No sooner had he hung up than his phone rang again. "I have to go. Will you call me when you hear anything?"

Phillip nodded, not really hearing anything at all anymore. All he seemed to be able to do was watch the door the doctor had come through, hoping that when he did again, it wouldn't be bad news. "Phillip." Dakota's voice caught his attention. "I'm going to get coffee. Would you like anything?" Phillip nodded his answer and Dakota walked away, leaving him alone.

There was nothing he could do, and Phillip found himself jumping as people entered and left the area. Getting up, he began to pace the floor, his nervousness taking over. He just wished someone would tell him something, anything. Dakota came back carrying a cup in each hand. Phillip took the one he offered, holding it in his hand, staring at it like he wasn't sure what to do with it. "He's going to be okay, Phillip. Haven's strong."

Phillip nodded. "I guess, but…." The door opened and the doctor walked over to them, looking tired.

"Is he going to be okay?" Phillip asked for what seemed like the millionth time.

"He came through the surgery. Although he died on the operating table, and we were able to revive him. Right now he's in ICU. His lungs were damaged and so were his kidneys. He'd bled quite a bit internally, but we were able to get it under control." The man released his breath slowly. "I'm guardedly optimistic, but the next day or so will tell the tale."

"Can we see him?" Dakota asked, and Phillip felt himself nodding, numb at the news.

"Yes. I'll tell the nurse to let you back one at a time, but you can only stay a few minutes. There's not much to see, I'm afraid. He'll be asleep at least the next twelve hours or so. He's been through a lot."

"Thank you, Doctor," Dakota said, and the man walked back through the doors, leaving them in the waiting room. Almost before he knew what was happening, Phillip found himself striding over to the receptionist station.

"Take the door right there," she said, pointing, "go up to the second floor, and follow the signs to ICU."

Phillip was on his way almost before she'd stopped talking. Dakota followed, but Phillip hardly noticed. Reaching the elevator, they rode up one floor and reached the intensive care unit, where they were directed to another waiting room. "They're getting him settled," the tall male nurse told them in the deepest voice Phillip had ever heard. "I'll come get you in a few minutes."

Phillip flopped into a chair. "I hate this part."

Dakota chuckled. "You were never very patient, if I remember."

Phillip glared back at Dakota. "I seem to remember a certain bone-jumping cowboy on a particular cruise a few years ago who wasn't particularly patient, either." Phillip felt his momentary smile fade as they watched the doors. The nurse returned, and Dakota motioned for Phillip to follow him.

"I'll wait here," Dakota said, picking up a magazine.

Phillip nodded his thanks to Dakota and followed the nurse through the doors and along a line of beds separated by curtains hanging from the ceiling. The nurse stepped to a bed, and Phillip followed, seeing Haven's black-and-blue face framed by a pillow. Phillip moved to stand beside the bed.

"You can only stay a few minutes," the nurse cautioned before moving away.

Phillip looked around at all the monitors. Tubes were connected to Haven's arm, and there were tubes in his nose. One even disappeared beneath the covers. Philip tried not to think where that one went. "I have so much I want to say to you," Phillip started to say as he saw a few of Haven's fingers peeking out from the bedding. Lightly touching the skin, Phillip stared at Haven, silently wishing for him to wake up. "Please be all right. I need you to get better." The monitor continued clicking, and Phillip saw what looked like a bellows moving up and down, realizing that was the one helping Haven breathe. "I love you, Haven, and I'm sorry it took this for me to tell you, and I'm sorry you're not awake to hear me say it. I never believed in God, not really, but if there is one, at least he'll know." Phillip leaned to one of the fingers, pressing a light kiss to the fingertip.

"That's all the time I can give you," the deep-voiced nurse said from behind him, and Phillip sniffled as he walked away from the bed and back out to the waiting room, where he collapsed in a chair. The nurse led Dakota back, and it seemed like just a few seconds before Dakota returned.

"We should go back to the ranch. There's nothing we can do right now," Dakota said to him, and Phillip nodded, hefting himself onto his feet, looking toward the door.

"I just don't want to leave him alone."

"We'll come back first thing in the morning. He needs his rest, and he'll be asleep for hours."

Phillip knew Dakota was right and forced his feet to move. It took a few minutes, but soon Phillip found himself out in the late-afternoon sunshine, but he hardly noticed it. Getting in the truck, Phillip looked up at the building, knowing that Haven was in there somewhere. Closing the door, Phillip said nothing the entire ride back to the ranch, not that he thought of anything in particular, either, other than Haven. He heard Dakota making phone calls on the periphery of his consciousness, but didn't pay any attention. Only the jostling of the truck as they pulled into the drive cut through his thoughts.

Phillip walked up the front steps and into the house. Wally had already gotten home and appeared to be making dinner. Phillip walked to his room, closing the door behind him. Flopping onto the bed, he found himself rolling onto the pillow Haven had used. He could still smell his lover's scent on the fabric. A soft knock sounded on the door and then it opened, Wally walking in. "Are you okay?"

"No, I'm completely stupid," Phillip answered.

Wally sat on the edge of the bed. "You're not stupid. You're my best friend and I love you," Wally said softly, as Phillip felt his hand on his side. "And for what it's worth, I believe in my heart that Haven's going to be okay." Phillip didn't know what to say to that. He certainly hoped to hell Wally was right. "You really shouldn't stay in here and mope, you know," Wally said, and Phillip felt the bed shift as Wally stood up. "Dakota's finishing dinner, and I could use your help."

Phillip sighed and sat up, rubbing his eyes. "What can I do?"

"Come on," Wally replied as he walked toward the door, "we have kitties who need their dinner."

"You've got to be kidding," Phillip grumbled as he nonetheless got off the bed, following Wally out to the barn and into his office area.

"They need fresh meat," Wally explained as he pulled open the door to one of the refrigerators, "but because I only have domesticated meat for them, they can't get everything they need." Wally hauled out a tray of red meat, placing it on the counter, before reaching up into one of the cabinets to get a huge bottle that rattled when he shook it.

"What are those?" Phillip asked as Wally placed six of the huge pills on the tray.

"Vitamins to help replace what they can't get." Wally handed him a knife, and Phillip wondered what in hell he was supposed to do. "Make a small, but deep, cut in the meat and shove in a pill. They'll eat them along with the rest." Wally demonstrated and Phillip followed along, preparing the dinner for one of the cats while Wally got the other two ready. "Do you want to talk?" Wally asked as he finished inserting the last pill.

"Not really. I think this is something I just have to work through by myself," Phillip answered as he finished with the last pill before following Wally out of the barn and onto the range behind the house.

"I'll have you feed Schian. He's much easier. Just motion with your hand, and he'll go to the far side of the enclosure. Lay the meat on his tray and shut the gate." Wally made it sound so damned easy. As they approached, Schian was standing in his area, looking every bit the king of the jungle; almost posed, he seemed so stately. Phillip did as Wally said, and Schian slowly moved to the far side of the cage. Sure enough, Phillip was able to open the door and set the meat on the tray. Schian didn't move until the gate closed again.

The tigers were a completely different matter. Philip watched as they both prowled the perimeter of their enclosures, smelling their dinner. Wally didn't come close, instead placing the meat on a metal grabber and sliding it through a slot high in the cage. The meat dropped onto the tray and the cat pounced on it. "Kahn thinks he's in the wild, but Sheba's not as difficult." Wally still used the pole to feed her, but she waited a distance away before descending on her food.

"Sheba looks like she's getting fat," Phillip commented as he watched the impressively beautiful cats. "Is she eating too much?"

"No." Wally stood beside him.

"See, look at her belly. She's thicker than Kahn and sort of round," Phillip said, pointing. "See near her back legs—watch when she sits." Phillip watched the cat eat, and then she got up, prowling around her enclosure again. Finally, after they'd watched her awhile, she sat down, watching them right back. "See what I mean?"

"Holy crap," Wally whispered under his breath, "or I should say, suffering cats, Sheba's pregnant." Wally looked again. "How on earth did you do that, girl?" he asked soothingly as he stepped a little closer to the enclosure, Sheba watching his every move. "I would have thought the circus would be aware of things like this," Wally continued as he turned back to Phillip. "Bengal tiger cubs are rare and incredibly valuable." Wally watched the tigers for a while before turning back toward the house. Phillip followed behind, his attention turning from the tigers back to Haven in the hospital. When they walked inside, Dakota had dinner on the table.

"The hospital just called. I gave them our number while you were visiting Haven. They said his condition has been upgraded from critical to serious. He hasn't awakened yet, and he's not out of the woods, but he's doing better," Dakota explained with a smile as he set the dishes on the table before bringing his father in to join them.

Phillip wasn't really hungry, but ate a little and waited for the others to finish, letting them talk while he felt himself retreating again into his own thoughts. "I'm going to go for a drive."

"Take one of the trucks," Dakota responded, tossing him a set of keys.

"Thanks, I'll see you all later." Phillip left the table, walking out to the truck. He drove the back roads, taking the route Haven had a few weeks earlier. Pulling off, he parked where, just a few days earlier, he and Haven had spent their first night together under the stars. Shutting off the engine, Phillip got out, looking up at the stars, the same ones he'd watched with Haven after their dinner, and the same ones they'd made love under that first night. "I was a fool, Haven. I should have told you how I felt, and I should have been honest with you and myself," he said out loud, listening to his own voice, hearing the cattle move around in the nearby range. "Jesus, now I'm talking to cows, or whatever they are," Phillip added with frustration at himself. Resting back on the hood of the truck, he felt the warmth of the engine seeping into his body as he looked up at the stars.

Phillip lost all track of time as he watched the points of light move slowly above him. He might have dozed for a few seconds; he wasn't really sure. Sliding off the hood, he got in the truck and drove back to the ranch. Most everything was dark when he arrived. Parking the truck, he quietly walked inside and to his room. Getting undressed, he slipped beneath the covers, hoping, but not hopeful, that he'd be able to sleep.

*Chapter Eleven*

HAVEN cracked his eyes and felt them grind like they were coated with sandpaper. Closing them again, he drifted back to sleep. He was happy, comfortable, and warm, his mind floated on clouds, and he had wings. Haven smiled to himself; he was an angel.

Pain and discomfort cut through him, and the clouds vanished. His wings disappeared and he fell back to earth. Cracking his eyes open again, he saw lights over him and heard strange beeps coming from around him. Nothing felt familiar, and he couldn't figure out where he was. Shaking his head slightly to try to clear away the fuzz that seemed to clog it, he moved his legs to try to stand, and searing pain shot through him. Instantly stilling, the pain dissipated, and he lay motionless, afraid to even breathe. "Honey, you're awake," a voice said from next to him. "Welcome back. We were worried about you." Haven tried to move his lips, but she shushed him. "Don't try to talk, just relax. You're going to be just fine. Are you in pain?"

Haven thought for a few minutes and nodded very slightly. By the second, he could feel more and more of his body screaming at him as pain built from slight discomfort to full-on, head-pounding, cut-off-my-arms-and-legs pain. "Hurts," he mumbled into the mask over his face, hoping that the voice could hear him.

"Okay, honey, I'll give you something."

Haven felt himself shaking, he hurt so bad, and he was convinced this was it and he was going to die. Closing his eyes again, he hoped he'd get those wings back, because it would mean he was dead and the pain would be over. Instead, it got worse.

"There you go—it'll take just a second." The voice wasn't kidding. Within no time at all, the pain was going away, and Haven opened his eyes again and found himself looking up at a tiled ceiling. A woman with a pleasant face appeared in his line of sight. "Is that better?" Haven nodded again and did his best to smile. "Good. You gave us quite a scare, but you're going to be fine. I'll be back to check on you in a little while, and you have a visitor to see you." She slipped away and the room got quiet. Haven tried to remember what had happened and concentrated as much as his clouded mind would allow.

"Haven," he heard what he thought was a familiar voice and turned his head slightly. Phillip stood next to his bed, and Haven blinked as everything came rushing back to him, the quarrel with Phillip, the trip into town, the fight, and then trying to drive home. "I'm sorry," Phillip said softly, and Haven felt a warm hand take his. "I shouldn't have let you go," Phillip said, and Haven wasn't sure what he was talking about, but the medication was definitely taking over, and he could feel his eyes getting heavy. "I was a fool," Phillip continued, and Haven thought he might be crying. He felt fingers stroking his hand, and then Haven's eyes closed and sleep claimed him.

When Haven woke again, there appeared to be sunlight coming in his window. He felt better. There was pain, but the nurse he remembered from before was there, smiling at him. He could move his neck a little, watching as she fiddled with tubes and machines. Slowly rolling his head to the other side, he saw someone sitting in a chair who looked to be asleep. "You slept well," she said. Haven blinked, and she leaned over the bed. "Let me take this mask off."

Haven stayed still as she removed the mask from over his face, replacing it with something just under his nose. When she was done, Haven rolled his head to the other side. A figure sat in the chair next to his bed, covered with a blanket. Haven blinked when he saw it was Phillip.

"He's been here for hours," the nurse said as she finished up and left the room. Haven lay and waited.

"Phillip," he said as pain shot through his throat. Haven swallowed, and it shot again, but this time it was definitely less.

"Haven." Phillip sat up and looked over at him with a smile. "How are you feeling?"

"Better, I guess," he rasped softly, his throat still aching.

"That's good. Do you know what happened to you?"

Haven now remembered that part very clearly. "Got into a fight with Herbie and his buddies."

Phillip nodded. "You're going to be okay now. Your lungs and kidneys were damaged, and they had to do surgery to fix them, but they said you'll get better now." Phillip's voice sounded so soft, and Haven looked into the eyes he knew he'd come to love and saw them fill with tears. "I was a stupid fool to ever let you walk away."

"Shhh, it's okay."

"No, it's not." Phillip took his hand and held it before kissing his knuckles lightly. "I should have told you how I felt. Haven, I should have told you I loved you."

Haven blinked a few times, making sure he was awake and that Phillip was really saying what he thought he was hearing.

"You love me?" Haven replied, and he felt a hand slide over his forehead.

"Yes, I love you, and I'm sorry it took you almost dying for me to realize it." Tears ran down Phillip's cheeks, and Haven felt as though he were going to cry as well. "I don't know what I'm going to do, but I decided last night as I was waiting for you to wake up that if you get better and if you'll have me, I'll try to find a job here. I don't know what I can do. I'm not really good at ranch work, but…."

Haven squeezed Phillip's fingers. "I love you too." Haven felt Phillip's lips touch his, and he knew this was real. Up till then he'd still thought it might have been a dream.

"Last night while you were here, I went up to that little hill where we first made love, and I thought of you. I kept wondering what my life would be like if I stayed here and what my life would be like when I went home, and I realized that if I went back, I wouldn't have a life because I wouldn't have you."

"I could sell the ranch and move back with you," Haven said softly, his throat still aching.

"No, I have friends here and someone who loves me here. If you want to sell the ranch, then you should sell it, but only if it's right for you. This is your home, and I want to try to make it my home too."

Haven yawned and found his eyes getting heavy again. Closing his mouth, Haven smiled, letting his eyes close again. As he drifted off to sleep, he could feel Phillip's warm hand in his. There were still so many things that needed to be done and worked through, but for now, Haven was content and happy. Phillip loved him and he was willing to stay. As sleep overtook him, Haven tried to keep it at bay just a little longer, trying to remember the last time someone had told him they loved him. It certainly hadn't been his father. Wracking his mind, he finally remembered—his grandfather had told him he loved him and so had his mother. Both were a long time ago, and somehow Haven knew it wouldn't be anywhere near as long before he heard those words again.

Sleep felt blessed, and the next time he woke, Haven found he felt better. Yes, he was still in pain, but he could move, and he at least felt warm. Haven immediately looked toward the chair next to the bed, but found it empty, and he wondered if he'd dreamed the entire conversation with Phillip.

"You're awake," Phillip said as he walked into the room carrying a cup of coffee. "You've been asleep for most of the afternoon and evening in addition to sleeping through the night. How do you feel?"

"Okay, I guess," Haven said, and he motioned toward the cup of water on his table. Phillip brought the straw to his lips so he could drink. "How long have I been here?"

"Almost two days," Phillip answered, setting the cup back on the roller table. "The doctor said you're doing as well as can be expected and you should be able to get out of bed in a few days."

"Phillip," Haven started to say and watched as the other man sat in the chair, "can I ask you something?"

"Of course." Haven felt the other man slide his hand into his.

"Did I wake up yesterday? Because if I didn't, I had the best dream ever." Haven tried to smile and hoped Phillip would tell him what happened.

"Haven," Philip said as his hand caressed the skin of Haven's palm, "are you asking me if you dreamed that I told you how I felt? Because you didn't." Phillip leaned closer, his face right next to Haven's, so close Haven could smell the heavenly aroma of the coffee on his breath. "I do love you, Haven."

Haven closed his eyes and said a little prayer of thanks. He'd hoped that had been real, because he was now pretty sure that the angels he'd seen in their little white wings, bare butts, with those magic hands, had been a dream. He just needed to make sure that his conversation with Philip hadn't been a dream as well. "What are we going to do?"

The hand in his gently began to move along his arm, Phillip's touch warming him in the nicest way. "First thing is that you need to get better. We'll worry about everything else when you're on your feet again."

Haven heard footsteps in the hall and saw Dakota and Wally enter his room. Wally had a big bunch of balloons, and Dakota carried a vase of flowers. "Before either of you say anything," Dakota said as he set down the vase, "that was Wally's idea. I wanted to bring you steaks."

Wally play-slapped the bigger man on the shoulder. "Then how come you insisted on the yellow flowers?" Wally rolled his eyes before turning to Haven. "How are you doing?"

"Better," Haven answered, and Phillip brought the straw to his mouth so he could drink again.

"That's really good," Wally added, sitting next to Dakota on the padded bench beneath the window. "The sheriff called and told us that Herbie's been arrested, along with the other two. Seems no one's buying their story that you started it. Besides, they have a history of this kind of thing. Seems they went into Cheyenne a few weeks ago and beat some guy up outside a bar so bad he may never walk again."

Haven looked over at Phillip. "I did start it, I guess. They were calling me names at the corner near your place, and I just sort of lost it, pulled Herbie from the truck before I saw the other two. Seems I didn't get very far before they had me on the ground. Thank God another truck came down the road, and they took off."

"How'd you make it to your truck and to Dakota's?" Phillip asked, his hand still in Haven's, and Haven found he really liked it there.

"Don't really know. All I remember after that is waking up here." God, he hated that, feeling like he was missing something, but not sure what or how to figure it out, anyway.

"Your truck's at your place. Kade came and got the supplies. He said he'll be up to see you later today," Dakota said from the bench. "I also had one of our men working with him to help out. So you don't need to worry about anything except getting better."

Haven saw Dakota's smile and wondered how he was ever going to pay the man back for all his kindness. Dakota, Wally, even Dakota's dad, had all been so good to him. "One thing I could never figure out is what it was between my father and Mr. Holden. Seems like they both hated each other, and Dad never told me why."

"I asked Dad," Dakota said, "and he clammed up tight. If you really want to know, maybe you need to be the one to ask him, because he won't tell me shit about it."

The conversation lulled, and everyone looked at one another, unsure what to say. "I've got some news," Wally said. "I was able to confirm today that Sheba's pregnant and that Kahn appears to be the father. We won't know for sure until the cubs are born, but that's how it looks. And it looks as though the Cheyenne Zoo is going to build a special exhibit for her and the cubs. She'll go to the zoo next week before she gets too far along," Wally said, beaming. "Bengals are endangered, so this will be great for the zoo and the species."

"Won't the circus want the cubs? After all, you got Sheba from them," Phillip asked, and Haven felt himself smile as the conversation swirled around, and he let his eyes drift closed, contented and happy.

Haven dozed and woke, dozed and woke, on and off for the rest of the afternoon. At some point, a tray appeared with gelatinous, tasteless food, and Haven ate what he could. Whenever he woke up, the people in the room with him seemed to change. Dakota and Wally left. Kade stopped in, as did some of his friends from school, and the lawyer handling his dad's estate came too. Through it all, Phillip stayed with him, a fixture sitting next to his bed, making sure he wasn't alone.

The doctor stopped in, greeting Haven. "I'm Dale Green. I operated on you a few days ago, and I just need to check how you're doing and change your bandages." He pulled the curtain and moved the blankets aside. Slowly, the doctor removed the bandage, and Haven got a look at the sizable incision that ran along one side. "It looks good. There's no unexpected swelling and the color looks right," Dr. Green commented as he lightly touched the skin, and Haven gasped a little. "I know it's tender, but I need to make sure it's getting the proper blood flow," he explained as he began re-bandaging the wound. "You're very lucky you got here when you did."

Haven stayed still and quiet as the doctor finished changing the bandage, replacing the blanket. "You'll be with us for a while yet, but you seem to be healing well, and there don't appear to be any signs of infection." The doctor put Haven's chart back in the container. "I'll stop by to see you again tomorrow. Is there anything you need?"

"Maybe some food that tastes like something."

The doctor smiled. "I'll see what I can do." With a smile as he drew the curtain back, Haven saw the doctor leave the room, and Phillip took his hand once more.

"You don't have to stay here all the time, you know. There have to be things you'd rather do besides sitting in that chair for hours on end."

"Well, actually, there is." Phillip looked toward the door and then leaned closer, touching their lips together. Haven felt Phillip's tongue slide over his lips, and for the first time in days, Haven felt himself becoming excited. He moaned softly, and for a second, Phillip deepened the kiss before slowly pulling his lips away. "I know we can't do more than that until you feel better, but I wanted to give you something to look forward to."

"You did," Haven answered as Phillip's lips slipped away. Sighing softly, Haven watched as Phillip stood up, walking toward the door. With a final wave and a smile, Phillip left the room, and Haven reached for the nearby remote, turning on the television.

FOR Haven, the days seemed to drag on. Phillip visited and spent a lot of time with him. Dakota, Wally, and Kade all came for visits, but with nothing to do, Haven was beginning to go out of his mind. The doctor started his latest visit the way he always did, by looking at his chart and checking his incision. "Well, you're doing well and getting stronger. I think we can send you home tomorrow."

Haven smiled and thanked the doctor as he pushed back the curtain and left the room, stepping out of the way as Phillip walked in. "I can go home tomorrow," Haven informed his boyfriend with a smile. "I have to take it easy, though, and I won't be able to work."

"You're not going to be able to take care of yourself, either, at least not for a few days," Phillip added with way too much glee. "So I guess you'll have to stay with me."

"What about the ranch? I can't just leave it. I've already been gone too long." Haven pressed the button to lift the head of the bed so he could see better. "Kade can't continue doing everything on his own."

"He's not. Dakota's had some of his men helping, and I've been over at your place when I'm not here, helping as best I can. Kade said to tell you that everything's fine and that he wants his best man up and healthy for his wedding." Phillip grinned as he sat in the chair next to the bed.

"What's in the bag?" Haven asked, his nose twitching, because he could smell something that was definitely not hospital food.

"I stopped at the diner on my way over," Phillip said as he set the bag on the tray. Haven reached in, pulling out the burger and taking a huge bite. The first taste of real food in days hit his tongue like a mini explosion, and Haven found himself eating ravenously. "I wanted to let you know that I finished going through all your dad's records and I didn't find much else except the usual things. I set it up so you can easily keep the records from now on. I can show you when you're ready."

Haven swallowed his bite of hamburger. "Did you find any place where Dad set anything aside for me?" He hadn't been holding out much hope, but he had to ask.

Phillip shook his head, touching the skin of his arm. "I'm afraid not. But I did at least find some notes he left in a locked drawer in his desk. I had to jimmy it to get it open. He was planning to put the ranch up for sale in the fall, and it looks like it would have brought a great deal of money." Haven continued eating as he listened to Phillip. "It seems your dad paid off the main mortgage on the property about the time he started squirreling money aside. There are operational loans and lines of credit to make sure you have cash when you need it, but other than that, you own the property free and clear."

"So what you're saying…." Haven swallowed before continuing, "Is that even though my dad was a greedy bastard, because he died when he did, he left me with a lot of money."

Phillip moved to the bed, sitting near Haven's feet. He loved that Phillip was so close, but worried about what it meant. "I did some calculations, and with the amounts of money that are involved, you could be talking about some serious inheritance taxes. There are provisions for family farms and ranches, but you need to be sure to cover all that with the lawyer. That's also why it's important to show where the money in your dad's accounts came from, because if we can demonstrate that half the cash should be yours, that comes off the table from your inheritance, and you pay less taxes. You also need to check how the property's deeded, because that may help you too."

Phillip was going a mile a minute, and Haven tried his best to keep up, but got completely lost. "Phillip, I don't understand all the parts about the money and taxes and stuff." Haven set down the rest of his food, his appetite slipping away. "My dad did all that. I took care of the cattle and made sure the ranch stayed in one piece."

Phillip touched his arm, a hand sliding until it rested in Haven's. "I know, and we can talk about this some more if you want, but I wanted you to know what you should ask your lawyer about."

"I'll never keep all this money stuff straight. I'm just a simple cowboy, and it's all I really want to do." Haven swallowed as the magnitude of what he was going to have to see to started to dawn on him. Up till now, he'd been able to push it aside, but that was no longer possible. "I don't know anything about that stuff…." Hell, he knew he sounded whiny, but that was all so overwhelming.

"It's okay, you don't have to. I'll help you with it, and I'll set things up so you can do what you need to do," Phillip said soothingly.

Haven swallowed and looked at Phillip, his mind going a mile a minute. "You mean when you're gone, don't you?" Haven folded his hands over his chest before lowering them again when they pulled on his side. "You said you loved me, but you're leaving!" Haven raised his voice for a second before remembering where he was.

"Haven," Phillip began, his voice soft and level. "I'll have to leave at least so I can get my things, but...." He stood up, walking over to the door, closing it quietly. "I didn't mean it that way. It's just I'm not going to replace your father and put you in the same boat he did. You realize the reason you don't know anything about how the ranch is run financially is because your dad didn't want you to." Phillip glared at him for a few seconds, and Haven looked down at the blankets on his bed. "I won't ever do that to you. And if you think for one minute that I'm going to work for you and live off of you, you are out of your mind." Phillip stepped closer, and Haven saw a touch of anger in Phillip's eyes. "I will get my own job and earn my own living. I'm not about to be kept by you or anyone else."

Haven continued staring at his blankets, picking at the edge of one of them. "I guess I thought you'd want to be with me and would help me with all that. I thought we'd do it together." Haven heard Phillip step closer.

"Haven, please look at me." Haven lifted his eyes to Phillip's. "I know you're a little scared right now, and I don't blame you, but if you want me to stay because you need help on the ranch, then you need to find someone to help you and pay them to do the job. I can't stay with you because you need help or want someone to take your father's place."

Haven didn't know what to make of what Phillip was saying. But could it be true? Haven didn't think so. He loved Phillip and wanted him with him. "That's not what I want. I'd like you to stay because you want to. Because you think you'll be happy here."

"I think I could be happy here with you," Phillip said, and Haven felt the knot in his stomach unwind a little. "But I need to have my own life," Phillip said softly before continuing, "that's not quite what I mean. If we're going to make this work, then I think we need to have our life together as well as parts of our life that are separate. I need to make my own living and pay my own way, and I can't do that if I'm working for you. And I think you need to rebuild the ranch the way you want it and make it yours. I can help, but that can't be what I do for a living. Do you understand?"

"I think so," Haven said tentatively, watching as Phillip opened the door to his room again. "Sort of like what Wally does. He has his own job, but he also takes care of the animals on the ranch."

"Exactly, I guess. What I'm saying is that I'll help you set up a system that will work for you, but you need to know what's happening and be able to do your own books and manage the ranch's money. As your partner, I'd help you, but I can't and won't do it for you. I won't leave you in the position your dad did. I love you too much for that."

Haven rested back on the bed smiling slightly, realizing for the first time just how much Phillip really did love him. And for the first time since his dad's death, Haven felt anxious and was even looking forward to getting back to work. He'd sat long enough in this hospital, and he'd retreated from his obligations at the ranch long enough. "Phillip, I was wondering…," Haven began. "I know I'm going to need some help when I go home tomorrow, and we talked about me staying at Dakota's for a few days, but I'd really like to go home. Dakota and Wally have been wonderful, but I think I need to go home."

Phillip's eyes narrowed. "Okay," he said skeptically, "we can do that, but if I catch you trying to work before you're fully healed, I'll tie you to the bed." Haven found himself staring at Phillip letting the zing of excitement run through him. The thought of Phillip tying him to his bed, making love to him, sent a thrill from his head to his toes. Phillip moved closer, his face near Haven's, their eyes meeting. "The thought of me tying you to the bed excites you, doesn't it?"

Haven's throat went dry, and he nodded slowly. He couldn't wait to go home and be alone with Phillip. Maybe they wouldn't be able to do much right away, but Phillips's deep voice slipped into his ear, and his hot breath caressed his neck, and Haven tried to form words, but couldn't.

"You have to say it, Haven," Phillip whispered into his ear.

He swallowed, turning his head toward Phillip as his body throbbed beneath the hospital blankets. "Yes," he managed to choke out as footsteps in the hallway brought back to mind where they were. Phillip moved away and sat back in the chair as an orderly came in, and Haven breathed a sigh of relief that the huge man didn't see his reaction to Phillip's proximity.

"I need to take you down for X-rays," he said, looking at both Phillip and Haven before unhitching the wheels on Haven's bed and taking him for a ride.

THE doctor had finally signed his release. Phillip had called and said he was on his way, so Haven waited, sitting on the edge of the bed. That morning was the first time he'd been able to sit up for a longer time, and it felt so good.

Finally, after what seemed like forever but couldn't have been more than ten minutes, Phillip walked in, followed by an orderly who helped him into a wheelchair. After gathering his things, he was on his way out of the hospital. Outside, Phillip pulled up the truck, and Haven walked slowly toward it with Phillip staying close by just in case. Getting in and shutting the door, Haven waited as Phillip stowed his things, and then walked around the back and got in the driver's seat before starting the truck and pulling away from the door. As they drove away, Haven turned around and looked as the hospital got smaller and smaller.

The drive home didn't take long, and soon Haven watched with a smile as the truck pulled into the ranch and came to a stop in front of the house. Phillip helped him out of the truck and up the steps into the house. "Let me sit on the sofa," Haven said, already tired from the short walk.

"You should get in bed," Phillip countered, and helped him down the hall. "I hope you like it." Phillip opened the door to his bedroom, and Haven gasped. The room had been changed. The small bed he'd always slept in had been removed. "I hope you aren't mad, but we thought that you probably weren't ready to move into the master bedroom, but...." Haven saw Phillip look at him nervously. "I thought if you wanted us to sleep together, we'd need something with a little more room."

"It's wonderful." Haven walked in and saw that the room had been painted, the scent still lingering, but only faintly.

"Yesterday when you asked to come home, I had to try to keep a straight face. I noticed that your bedroom still looked like it probably has for years and thought you deserved something a little nicer. All your things are in the closet." Phillip opened the door, showing Haven the neatly stacked and labeled boxes. "If you don't like the color, we can repaint, but I thought a nice blue would work." Phillip's words tumbled out nervously as he led Haven toward the bed.

"Where did you get all the stuff?"

"The bed frame came from Wally, along with the matching dresser, and the linens I bought in town. I hung your pictures on the walls." Phillip walked to the dresser, and Haven saw the only picture he had of his mother hanging above, framed and everything, along with two others that he'd never seen before.

"Where did you get those?" Haven asked, his eyes going wide as he gingerly sat on the edge of the bed.

"I told Dakota's dad that you didn't have many pictures of your mom, and the next day he handed me those and told me to give them to you. When I asked him about them, he clammed up tighter than a drum," Phillip added before kneeling on the floor and helping Haven out of his shoes. "Later, after you've rested, I'll be happy to help you put back any of your things you want."

Haven swallowed as he looked over the room. Phillip and his friends had gone to a great deal of trouble to do this for him, and the room looked so nice. "Thank you."

"You like it?"

"Yes, I really do," Haven said softly as he felt the last of his energy start to ebb away. Phillip helped him out of his clothes and pulled back the covers. Settling on the sheets, Phillip pulled up the covers before kissing him lightly. "Rest now. I'll be here when you get up, I promise."

Haven smiled and nodded, his eyes already heavy, and almost as soon as Phillip left the room, Haven fell into a deep sleep. He woke what must have been hours later, the light coming in the windows turning a light shade of pink. Voices came from the living room, and Haven slowly got out of bed, slipping on the robe he found draped over the end of the bed.

"Hey, sleepyhead," Dakota said with a smile as Haven walked into the living room. Phillip jumped up and helped him to the sofa. "How are you feeling?"

"Tired but good, I guess."

"Phillip said you liked the room."

Haven grinned. "I really did." Haven looked to Wally and Kade as well as Phillip. "Thank you all. It was a great coming-home present. Especially the pictures of my mom," he said, looking at Dakota, figuring he must have had something to do with them.

"What pictures of your mom?" Dakota asked, clearly confused.

Phillip explained, "I happened to mention to your dad in passing a few days ago that Haven only had one picture of his mom, and the next day your dad gave me some."

"Could I see them?" Dakota asked.

"Of course, they're hanging on the wall in the bedroom," Haven answered, wondering what was going on. Getting up, he slowly followed, with Phillip hanging onto his arm like he was some sort of invalid. Granted, Haven figured he'd never get tired of the man touching him, so he let it go.

Dakota stood in front of his dresser, intently studying the photographs. "I wonder where my dad had these? Over the last few years, with his MS and all, I've had to do almost everything for him, and I thought I'd been through everything, but these I've never seen." Dakota looked toward Haven and then back at the pictures.

"I thought it strange that your dad had pictures of my mom. Maybe before whatever happened to make our fathers hate each other so much, they were friends or something," Haven mused as he watched Dakota's expression alter from confused to shocked. "What is it?" Haven asked as he stepped into the room.

"These pictures," Dakota said, stepping closer. "They were taken in our house. Look," he said, pointing, "that sofa she's sitting on, I remember it because I used to jump on it as a kid because it was really springy. See?" Dakota moved his finger. "That picture is now in my dad's room."

"Why's that so strange?" Phillip asked from next to him. "If they were friends like Haven suggested, then it wouldn't be unusual for them to have visited and for your dad to have pictures."

"No, it wouldn't, except in this picture," Dakota said, moving to the other photograph, "you see that man in the background watching your mother with such adoration?"

"Yeah, I saw that, but figured it was my dad, why?" Haven stepped closer to get a better look.

"That's not your dad. It's my dad." Dakota turned, looking at him, face completely serious.

"Dakota," Phillip said, "your dad could be looking at someone else."

Dakota shook his head, looking closer at the photograph. "No, he's looking intently at Haven's mom." Dakota shuddered as the implications sank in around the small room. "Maybe now he'll tell me about it," Dakota mumbled softly, and Haven placed his hand on Dakota's arm.

"No, and you shouldn't ask him," Haven said, and Dakota began to argue, but Wally cut him off with one look.

"Haven's right. It's none of your business. Would you want to discuss your youthful indiscretions with your son? I don't think so," Wally said firmly. "Besides, you know dang well your dad can be just as stubborn as you and won't tell you anything he doesn't want to." Wally looked to him. "If Haven wants to ask Jefferson about it, then that's his business, but you need to stay away from it. Besides, you could be all wrong, and then you'd just make your dad feel bad, and you'd feel stupid."

"It wouldn't be the first time," Dakota replied, obviously curious, but he finally let his gaze drift away from the pictures. "We should get going."

"Dakota," Haven said as they walked back down the hall, and Dakota stopped, with the others filing past and into the living room. "In a few days, when I'm feeling better, would you come over? I think I'd like to talk to you."

Dakota seemed to study him before nodding slightly. "Sure."

"Thanks, I need your advice, but I'm not up to it right now."

Dakota smiled. "Okay, I'll come over in a few days, and we can talk." Dakota turned around to join the others.

"Wally's right. Your dad deserves his privacy," Haven said, thinking Dakota hadn't let things go.

"Don't you want to know about your mother?"

"Yes, but your dad will tell when he's ready, and he isn't yet," Haven answered, but truth be known, he was dying to know if there was more to the story or not. But it wasn't his place to ask, and it certainly wasn't Dakota's.

"What if he's never ready?"

Haven stepped closer, lowering his voice. "I've already got more than I had before—he gave me those pictures of my mother."

Dakota looked as though he was about to argue, but then his expression changed. "You're a good man, Haven. You really are."

Dakota continued to the living room, with Haven following more slowly.

Kade walked toward the door. "I'm going to get back to work," he said, looking at Haven. "I'll stop by in the morning, and we can discuss where things are and what you'd like to get done first."

"We should be going too," Wally said, and after both Wally and Dakota gingerly hugged him, they said their goodbyes and left, leaving him and Phillip alone.

"You should go back to bed," Phillip said softly. "I made some dinner while you were sleeping. I'll bring a plate in for you."

"I've eaten enough meals in bed to last me a while. I'll sit on the sofa and eat at the coffee table with you before going back to bed." To his surprise, Phillip didn't argue, and they had a quiet pasta dinner together. Afterward, Phillip did the dishes, and Haven, following orders, walked down the hall to his room. Slipping under the covers, he listened to the soft domestic sounds that filtered through the house.

"You should be asleep," Phillip said with a smile from his doorway.

"I'm not really tired," Haven answered, patting the bed next to him. "But I could use some company."

Phillip smiled and slipped out of his shoes, walking around to the other side of the bed. Haven lifted the blankets and heard Phillip gasp slightly when he saw him.

"You're naked," Phillip said, and Haven slipped the covers down further, his cock standing at attention, and Phillip grinned widely. "And horny."

"Uh-huh," Haven replied, desperately hoping Phillip would take the hint. Phillip smiled and his eyes darkened, and Haven felt his heart pound faster as Phillip's shirt slipped off his shoulders. Then the rest opened, and Phillip's pants slid down his legs.

"I'm not sure you're ready for this yet," Phillip said softly, "but I know I've missed you terribly." Phillip's underwear slipped over his smooth butt, and Haven reached out, his fingers trailing over Phillip's skin. The bed shifted as Phillip slipped in next to him. "I'm afraid of hurting you."

"You'd never hurt me. I know that," Haven said soothingly. He slid his hands over Phillip's chest and stomach as their mouths met in a hungry kiss that continued until Haven was short of breath. "I've thought about that for days," Haven confessed just before going in for another kiss, and Haven felt Phillip's hands slide along his skin, fingers briefly encircling his erection before slipping away again.

Phillip actually smiled when Haven groaned in frustration. "We really shouldn't be doing this. You just got home from the hospital, and you need to rest and get better."

Haven tugged Phillip's head closer, kissing the unwanted words away. He needed this. He'd been in the hospital for more than a week—with nothing much to do besides think of Phillip's hands on his body and what Phillip would feel like inside him. "What'll make me better is you."

"Okay," Phillip said, stopping his hands and moving away from him, getting off the bed as he breathed steadily. "But we do this my way, and you have to promise me you'll say something at the first sign of pain."

Haven was ready to agree to just about anything if it would get Phillip's hands back on his skin. "Okay, I promise, Scout's honor," Haven said, holding up his right hand, while his left wrapped itself around his dick.

Phillip scowled at him. "That's enough of that," he commanded, looking at Haven's hand, and he pulled it away with a groan, the firmness in Phillip's voice sending a shiver through him. "Like I said, we're doing this my way. I want you to lie on your back with your hands at your side." Haven complied, his entire body quivering with unabashed desire. Phillip moved closer, his hands lightly stroking the skin of his stomach. "I'm serious, if you feel any pain, we have to stop. The last thing I want is for you to get hurt."

"I want you so bad," Haven moaned softly as fingers lightly flicked over a nipple.

"I know you do, and I want you just as badly." Phillip leaned forward, his tongue sliding over Haven's chest, lips lightly sucking. Haven heard the drawer opening and turned to see what was happening. "Look at me," Phillip admonished, and Haven shifted his gaze back, concentrating on what Phillip was doing, forgetting everything else, and when Phillip's lips slid over the crown of his cock, thoughts of anything except a momentary vision of heaven flew from his mind.

"Phillip," Haven moaned, and he bucked forward, and then felt a light swat on the leg.

"You can't do that," Phillip admonished lightly before moving away, to Haven's total dismay.

"Do you want me to roll over so you can fuck me?" Haven asked, already flipping himself onto his stomach.

"No, Haven," Phillip answered, lightly rolling him back. "You just have to remember not to move." Then Phillip leaned closer, lips tugging on his ear. "Oh, I'm going to fuck you," Phillip said, his voice deep and throaty, "but not today. What I have in mind for then is a little too athletic for you to take right now. So put your hands at you side and lie back."

Haven did as he was told, watching every move Phillip made as he climbed on the bed, knees resting on the mattress. Phillip's eyes bored into his, and Haven barely heard a soft snick, but he saw Phillip squirt something in his fingers before reaching around behind himself. Haven's mind tried to imagine what he was doing. Phillip opened a condom, and Haven gasped as he felt Phillip's fingers on him followed by a slick coolness. Then Phillip settled back, and Haven's eyes widened and his mouth fell open in a silent cry as he felt Phillip's hands on him and he slipped into molten heat unlike anything he'd ever imagined.

Phillip cautioned him to stay still as Haven felt himself slide deeper and deeper into his lover's body. The sensations were unimaginable as he felt Phillip take him in. "You have to let me do the work," Phillip said with a gasp, as Haven felt his lover's butt against his hips.

"But Phillip," Haven whined as his body screamed at him to move.

"I know, but you have to let me," Phillip said as he lifted himself up and then lowered his body again to a chorus of groans from both of them. "Damn, you feel so good inside me."

Haven felt Phillip slowly rise and descend, each time stealing his breath away. Testing the waters a little, he thrust forward and felt no pain, only pleasure and the tight, slick heat of Phillip's body. Haven began thrusting with more vigor and felt his skin tighten slightly. Haven forced himself to back off and let Phillip take charge again, riding the waves of unimagined pleasure that Phillip's body provided. "Phillip, I need...."

"I know," Phillip said, resting on his hips to still them while Haven felt Phillip's body squeezing him like a vise. "Imagine how this is going to feel when I have you all tied up so you can't move, and I'm the one buried deep inside you, filling you up, fucking you so hard you forget your own name," Phillip growled as he lifted up and bore back down. "Have you ever wondered how it'll feel to have your legs encased in leather chaps, bent over the bed, your ass exposed, while I'm riding you into the sunset?"

Haven groaned at the thought, surprised at how Phillip's dirty talk turned him on almost as much as his body's grip on his. "Where will we...." Haven gasped as Phillip took him deep once again, and he felt his body shake, as everything around him fell away with an overwhelming need to come. Nothing else mattered, and Haven found himself thrusting as hard as he dared, crying out as Phillip pressed him back against the mattress.

"Or maybe," Phillip groaned as his fingers plucked Haven's nipples, "you'd like a pair of clamps on these, squeezing just right. Your little nipples would look beautiful in a pair of little gold clamps."

The very idea felt so sinfully wicked Haven could no longer control himself, and as Phillip lowered himself again, Haven felt his release overtake him, and with a room-filling shout, came deep and hard, constellations flashing behind his eyes. Peeling them open as his orgasm subsided, Haven saw Phillip leaning back, hand stroking fast, eyes closed as he made these incredible small noises that filled the room. Haven's breath caught as Phillip's grip on him tightened and he came, painting ribbons onto Haven's skin.

Haven lay in the world's most relaxed state, Phillip's weight still on his legs, their bodies connected. Slowly, he felt Phillip's weight lift off him, and he sighed, closing his eyes as their bodies separated. Stepping off the bed, Phillip stumbled to the bathroom, returning a little steadier on his feet with a cloth. After cleaning him up, Haven watched as Phillip came back, slipping in with him beneath the sheets. "That was amazing," Haven murmured softly into Phillip's ear. "You took my breath away."

"You aren't hurt, are you? You seemed a little active there for a while," Phillip whispered in response, and Haven felt the other man curl next to him.

"No, I'm fine, better than fine. Actually, I feel better than I have in a long time." Haven yawned as the exertion caught up with him. "I think I can sleep now." Haven rested his head against Phillip's shoulder. "I don't know what more to say."

Phillip turned toward him, looking confused. "About what?"

"Well, while I was in the hospital and had a lot of time to think, I sort of realized that my dad never really loved me. All those years after Mom left, there was just the two of us, and it's hard for me to remember him ever giving me a kind word. He certainly never told me he loved me." Haven swallowed. "And then a few days ago, I woke up in the hospital, and you were there, and you told me you loved me, and you've done nothing since then but demonstrate that."

Haven felt Phillip's hand on his cheek. "How could anyone get to know you and not love you?" Phillip moved closer, kissing him so softly. "Your dad was a complete ass if he didn't see what a wonderful person you were. In fact, your dad didn't deserve you. So, yes, I love you, Haven Jessup, and while I don't know what the future will bring, I'll do my best to make it a good one." Phillip brushed his cheek again. "Go to sleep. There will be plenty of work, and you'll need your rest."

"When were you planning to go back for your stuff?" Haven asked, yawning, his eyes already heavy.

"I haven't given that much thought yet. We'll talk about things tomorrow, I promise."

Haven nodded and let sleep overtake him as he listened to the sound of Phillip's steady breathing.

*Chapter Twelve*

FOR two days, Phillip somehow managed to keep Haven inside, but this morning, the man was up at the crack of dawn and dressed before Phillip even had his first cup of coffee. Phillip watched him through the window, smiling as Haven walked around, looking at everything. Phillip dressed and walked outside, catching Haven's eye. "I know," Haven said as he walked over to where Phillip stood on the porch drinking his coffee. "I won't try to lift anything, I promise." Haven continued coming closer, and Phillip felt his body react to the man's proximity. Healed or not, Haven was insatiable when it came to making love. "I have to go over to see Dakota later this morning. There're some things I want to talk over with him."

Phillip wanted to ask what they were, but hid his curiosity behind his coffee mug. If and when Haven wanted him to know, he'd tell him. "Do you want me to come too?"

"Of course," Haven answered as he climbed the stairs. "I'd like your opinion as well." Haven leaned close for a kiss before walking back down the stairs and out toward the paddocks. Haven still favored the side that had the surgery. No one else would notice, but Phillip did. Finishing his coffee, Phillip finished dressing before joining Haven in the yard as he leaned against the fence of Jake's paddock.

"Have you thought of getting a new horse?" Phillip asked softly as he joined him, slipping an arm around Haven's waist. "I know you miss Jake."

"I do," Haven said, turning toward him. "That's one of the things I sort of want to talk to Dakota about."

"I don't understand," Phillip said as he watched the expression on Haven's face. "You've been so pensive for the last few days. Is something wrong?"

Haven shook his head slowly. "Not really. I've been doing a lot of thinking for a while, and I've come to some decisions, but there are so many things I don't know." Haven looked up at him. "I just don't feel quite ready to talk about it yet. It's not you. It's just that the idea's still forming." Haven fell quiet, and Phillip stood next to him, doing his own thinking. If he was going to stay, he needed to find a job.

"I wonder if there are any businesses in the area that need an accountant?" Phillip wondered out loud, and thought he should begin making the rounds around town to see if his skills were in demand. He certainly couldn't stay around the ranch doing nothing, and he didn't know the first thing about running a ranch—that was for damn sure. As he thought, he remembered that Jefferson had told him to ask Dakota and Wally. *Why was it that everything here involved those two?* Smiling to himself, Phillip made an internal note to ask Dakota what Jefferson meant.

The morning passed surprisingly quickly, and to Phillip's relief, Haven seemed to have his energy back. He noticed that he seemed to flag a little at lunchtime, but food seemed to revive him. "Is everything the way you want it?" Phillip asked Haven as he put a plate of sandwiches on the table for Haven and Kade.

"Yes," Haven said taking a sandwich and bumping Kade's shoulder. "I'm going to miss this guy when he leaves. He and Dakota's guys did a great job. They even got the paddock fence repaired, which is something I've been trying to get to for a while, but we never got around to."

Kade reached for a sandwich, taking a huge bite from one corner. Phillip swore both men inhaled their food rather than ate it. "This afternoon, I thought we'd do those fence repairs in the south range," Kade said between bites.

"Do you need help?" Haven asked, and Phillip shot him a look before turning away. He wasn't Haven's mother and couldn't watch over him like that. But damn, he just wanted to take the man back to bed and make sure he rested and healed fully.

"No, we've got it. There's just a few posts that need to be replaced, and I thought I'd replace the old wood ones with metal—that way we wouldn't have to do it again." Kade took another sandwich from the plate, and Phillip sat down, listening to the two men talk, not understanding much of it and feeling sort of like an outsider. He didn't know anything about ranching. *How in the hell was he ever going to fit in here?* Phillip reached for a sandwich, taking a small bite before setting the rest of it on his plate. Yes, he loved Haven, that he was sure of, but was he rushing into things? He'd only been here a few weeks and already he was getting ready to uproot his life and move across the country. Kade and Phillip continued to talk. Phillip slowly ate, watching them completely engrossed in a discussion about rangeland and the better ways to keep the cattle watered without impacting the long-term health of the land.

Phillip sat and listened, not understanding crap. Taking a deep breath, he silently let it out, looking around the room. *Was this going to be his life, taking care of the cooking and keeping the house while Haven worked? That certainly wasn't what he wanted, but what else could he do?* Yes, he could help Haven with the books, but that was hardly enough to fill his days. A hand on his leg pulled Phillip out of his thoughts, and he saw Haven smile at him, the hand squeezing just so, Haven's eyes lighting up in a way all that ranch talk hadn't made him do. "Phillip and I will be at Dakota's for most of the afternoon, so if you need anything, call my cell."

Kade grinned. "Good. You shouldn't do too much right away. I can handle the fence." Kade finished what had to be his fourth sandwich before getting up and placing his dishes in the sink. "I'll call you when I'm done, and maybe we can check on the herds when you get back."

Haven shook his head. "I don't really know when we'll be back. So go ahead and do the herd checks. I'll call you when I get done and hopefully I can help."

"We got it, don't worry," Kade said with a smile before heading out to work. As the front door opened Phillip heard Kade calling to one of the men Dakota had sent over to help. Taking away Haven's empty plate, Phillip ran some water to get the dishes done.

"I got that," Haven said with a grin as he rolled up his sleeves, quickly doing the dishes.

Phillip stepped away, sitting on one of the kitchen chairs. "I don't know what to do with myself. I'm not a ranch hand, and quite frankly, I don't want to be. I like being an accountant and working with numbers." Phillip sighed loudly. "Yes, I like riding a horse, but not for hours on end the way you do. I just don't know how I'm ever going to fit in here."

Phillip saw Haven's shoulders slump, his hands still in the dishwater. "You want to go home, don't you?" Haven turned to look at him.

"Haven, I have to be useful, and I don't see that yet." Phillip got up, stepping behind Haven and slipping his arms around his waist, resting his head on his back. "No, I really don't want to go back. I like it here. It's different, but I think we can have a good life together. I just need to feel useful." Phillip knew he was probably whining a little, but he needed his lover to understand.

Haven turned in his arms. "I know you do, and I want you to. I think part of what I like about you is that you aren't a ranch person. You've seen things outside of this ranch and this town. I know there's more to the world than this ranch and horses and cattle. I love being a cowboy, but I also love that you aren't one." Haven kissed him lightly before returning to the sink. "Let me get these dishes done and we can go. Maybe Wally and Dakota will have some ideas."

"A few days ago, Jefferson suggested I talk to those two as well," Phillip said. "It's funny how everything here seems to revolve around them. Have you noticed that?"

Haven turned on the water to rinse the dishes. "Well, not everything," Haven said with a leer that had Phillip's blood racing.

"You're turning into some sort of perv, aren't you?" Phillip asked as he returned Haven's look. "Not that I'm complaining."

Haven scoffed as he turned off the water. "That's the pot calling the kettle black, don't you think?" Haven said as he wiped his hands and stepped away from the sink. "Wally told me about your toy closet back home," Haven confessed, and Phillip saw the little shiver that went through his lover.

Phillip smiled and forced his mind away from a vision of how Haven would look all tied up with his toys on him and in him. "That's enough, or we'll never get out of here." Phillip followed Haven toward the front door. "There is one thing that just has to change," Phillip said with a smile.

"And what is that?"

Phillip waved his hands around the living room. "The old tumbledown-furniture look and nineties curtains just have to go." He saw Haven's eyes narrow. "I'm not being mean, and I don't mean we should citify the place," Phillip said, smirking. "Heaven forbid," he added teasingly and saw Haven smile. "But we should make it nicer and a little more fitting of both of us." Phillip stepped to where Haven had stopped. "Make it a place where we're both comfortable, sort of like the bedroom."

"I've got some horns in the barn. We could hang those on the walls," Haven said. "They'd look really nice over the doors."

"There are—" Phillip started to say, and then he saw Haven's wicked grin. Phillip made a leap for Haven, and he ducked out the front door, laughing at the top of his lungs as he tried to make it to the truck. "Let's go, ya goof," Phillip said, grinning when he reached the truck. "You didn't hurt yourself, did you?" Haven shook his head, still grinning like an idiot. Phillip climbed in the truck and held out his hand for the keys before driving the short distance to the ranch next door.

"HEY, Dakota," Haven called as they got out of the truck.

"Hi, Haven, hey, Phillip," Dakota called back as he swung a bale of hay into the back of his truck, the pack of dogs that formed the welcoming committee bounding around the two men's legs, looking for scratches. "Go on in. I'll just be a minute."

Phillip handed out scratches and got a good case of tail-lash on his legs before heading into the house. Jefferson sat in the living room with the television on, asleep in his wheelchair. They tried to be quiet, but Phillip saw him jerk awake almost as soon as they entered the room. "We didn't mean to wake you," Haven said, greeting the man with a smile.

"I can nap anytime," Jefferson said, a smile forming on his face. "Did Dakota see you?"

"He said he'd be right in," Phillip answered, sitting on the sofa as the door opened and both Dakota and Wally walked in.

Dakota greeted his dad and then wheeled him down the hall, both of them returning a while later. "Dad, Haven and I have some things to discuss. Will you keep Phillip entertained for a while?" Dakota asked, with a wink in Phillip's direction.

Phillip nodded, and Dakota led Haven into his office. "Since the warden's left," Phillip said, referring to Dakota, "would you like a beer?" Without waiting for an answer, knowing he didn't need one, Phillip went to the refrigerator. "Wally, do you want one too?"

"I'd love one, but I can't. I'm on call and may need to drive," Wally called in from the other room as a phone rang. "See? Right on time," Wally said as Phillip came back in the room, and two seconds later, the man was out the door and on his way to his truck.

"I guess it's just you and me," Phillip said to Jefferson, handing him a beer before sitting on the sofa. "I haven't had a chance to tell you, but Haven loved the pictures of his mom."

Jefferson took a swig of his beer before slowly lowering the bottle. "Dakota's mother died when he was still young. I loved her more than anything, but she died and left me with a son to raise." Jefferson stared at the television as he spoke. "A few years later, I met Nadine, Haven's mother. I knew she was Jessup's wife, and I tried my best for it not to happen, but we fell in love. For the longest time, we fought it, only seeing each other at the holidays. Jessup and I weren't close friends, but we were always neighborly and got along. After a while, Nadine told me that she wasn't happy and hadn't been in a long time." Jefferson took another drink from his beer, and Phillip sat as still as he could, afraid to break the spell. "Haven must have been about seven when she told me she was leaving Jessup, and we began a short affair. I'd been alone with just Dakota for years by that point, and in my defense, I did love her." Jefferson's voice began to slur, but his eyes appeared clear and bright.

"One night after we'd been seeing each other for a few months, she told Jessup that she was leaving him. He flew into a rage and tried to beat her, but she ran out of the house and came to me. Jessup followed her and confronted her, accusing her of having an affair, and neither of us denied it—there was no point. After he left, at near gunpoint, I told her I'd stick by her regardless, but she said no and made preparations to take Haven with her and get out of town."

"I take it she couldn't," Phillip said softly.

"No. Jessup wasn't letting go of his son, and threatened to crucify both her and me in any custody hearing." Phillip saw a tear run down Jefferson's face. "She came to me that night and stayed while we tried to figure out what to do. But the next morning, she was gone."

Phillip felt his mouth fall open when he realized what she'd done. "She left Haven?" He could hardly believe what he was hearing. *What kind of mother left her child?*

"She left a note explaining that she was going to try to find a place to live and would come back to get her son. She asked me to help her when the time came. It never did." Jefferson swallowed hard before sipping his beer. Phillip wondered if Jefferson might be drinking too much but figured if the man needed a little fortification after what he'd just told him, he deserved it. Shifting slightly in the chair, Jefferson motioned toward the top dresser drawer, and Phillip reached in, pulling out what looked like three envelopes. "The top one is the one she left for me the last night I ever saw her."

Phillip didn't open it, figuring it was private, and he slipped that one back into the pouch. "That one I got about two weeks later, saying she was okay and had gotten a job. The last one arrived about a month later and was addressed to Haven." Phillip turned it over and saw it had never been opened. "I've wondered what to do with that letter for years." Jefferson's voice was becoming rapidly harsh, and Philip knew he'd probably talked too much. "I think it's time he got it."

"You should give it to him," Phillip said handing the letter back, but Jefferson shook his head just a little.

"No," he said softly, "I can't tell that story again. I've spent the last fourteen years missing Nadine almost as much as I've missed my Daisy. I've been so ashamed of the way I acted. If I'd have just said no, that boy would still have his mama."

"You don't know that. If she was that unhappy, she'd have left anyway," Phillip replied softly. "All you can know for sure is that you made her happy for a little while." Phillip moved closer. "Do you know what happened to her?"

"Yes," Jefferson answered but didn't say any more, and Phillip thought he was done. "She made it as far as Las Vegas and ended up on the streets. After I got the first letter, I saw the postmark and followed her. She was working in a seedy casino as a stripper, and I later found out as a call girl. I didn't approach her, and she didn't approach me, but she saw me, I know she did, because a week later the letter to Haven arrived. A few years later, I found out she'd died not long after sending Haven's letter." The tears were coming regularly now, and Phillip pulled a tissue from the table and wiped Jefferson's eyes. "I'll leave it up to you what you want to tell Haven, or Dakota, for that matter."

Phillip swallowed. "Why me?"

"Because I know you'll do what's right for everyone," Jefferson said, and then sat quietly. Phillip got up to get another beer, he needed one, touching Jefferson's shoulder reassuringly on the way. Opening the refrigerator door, Phillip took out a bottle, popped it open, and took a huge gulp before taking a second. Finally saying to hell with it, he finished it off and threw the empty into the trash, closing the refrigerator door.

Walking down the hall, Phillip went into the room he'd been using, got his suitcase, and put the letter in one of the pockets. Taking the opportunity, he packed up the last of his things into the suitcase and took it with him to the living room. He found Dakota and Haven sitting with Jefferson, watching the game.

Phillip walked behind Haven, touching his shoulder as he leaned over the back for a kiss, which he got, with tongue, even. "I take it your conversation went well," Phillip commented with a smile.

Haven turned, and Phillip saw his ear-to-ear grin. "Yeah, it did. We'll tell you all about it once Wally gets back." Haven seemed to bounce on the sofa, he was so excited. Phillip wondered what could make Haven so happy, but whatever it was, he was definitely in favor. Joining the other men in the living room, he half watched the game, spending more time watching Haven. If Wally didn't get here soon, Haven was going to bust a gut. After an additional hour of Haven squirming and Dakota grinning like the cat that ate the canary, Wally's truck pulled into the drive.

Both Dakota and Haven jumped to their feet as soon as Wally walked inside, and Phillip chuckled lightly, seeing the two grown men behaving like kids. "What's going on?" Wally asked as Dakota practically tugged him into the room and down onto the sofa. "What's got you so excited?" Wally laughed as Dakota gave him a quick kiss.

"Haven and I were talking," Dakota started to say.

"Yes, I know. You were doing that when I left. Did you make some decisions?" Wally asked Dakota, and Phillip found himself totally confused.

"Okay, there's obviously more than one thing going on here," Phillip said, turning to Dakota, "so spill it. You seem to be the one at the center of all this."

Dakota looked to Wally and then Haven before starting. "Well, it seems that a number of things have come together, so I think I'll explain." Dakota then leaned close to Wally and said, "But to answer your question, yes, I have made a decision." Dakota looked up toward the rest of them. "Now everyone sit still, and I'll try to explain. Haven came over today to ask me about buying his ranch. It seems that Haven's happiest being a cowboy and isn't really interested in running his own ranch."

Phillip felt his mouth fall open, and he looked at Haven. "You're actually going to sell your ranch?"

"Just a minute, let Dakota finish," Haven responded, still very excited, before looking to Dakota so he could continue.

"There were a few problems with that, not least of which is the fact that I don't have the money to buy Haven's ranch without taking on a shitload of debt, which I won't do. So we talked about something else." Dakota turned to his dad who seemed to be listening intently. "What we'd like to do is merge the properties. Incorporate them into one large entity. We already know that the little guys in this business often don't last long, but together we'd be one of the larger operations in this part of the state. Haven has plenty of land. In fact, some of it hasn't been used in a while, so it'll be fresh, and we can expand. We have land as well as water, and the men to run the whole operation."

Phillip caught on quickly. "So you two are going to go into business together?"

"There are still details to work out, but we think this could make us more successful than either of us is now. Haven would run the cattle operation along with Mario, but he'd be the boss of that part of the business. And we'd need a business manager. Haven and I both agreed that if you're willing, we'd like to offer you the job," Dakota said, looking squarely at Phillip. "We'll need someone with excellent financial and accounting skills."

"But what about you?" Phillip asked. "Aren't you going to have a role in this?"

"Not directly, no. Between Haven, Mario, and you, if you take the job, the business should be in very good hands." Dakota looked at Wally. "To answer the question we talked about last night, yes." Wally smiled back at Dakota.

"What question?" Jefferson asked softly.

Dakota knelt next to his father's wheelchair. "If it's okay with you, I've decided to go back to medical school. Wally has said he'd support me if I want to do it, and this arrangement will make that possible. I'd attend school in Casper, so I wouldn't be too far away, and I could commute some of the time. It'll be harder on you because I won't be here to take care of you as much. That'll mean more nurses rather than me."

"That's all I've ever wanted for you," Jefferson said, his voice rough, but he was obviously pleased. "I'll be fine, Dakota. You need to get on with your life." Jefferson lifted his good hand, putting it around Dakota's neck, hugging his son as best he could.

"What kind of doctor are you going to be?" Haven asked.

"I've decided to be a good old-fashioned country doctor. It'll take a little extra time because I'll have to repeat some of my first-year classes, but I should be able to complete medical school in a few years. It's going to mean me being away for long stretches of time." Dakota looked at Wally. "Are you sure that's okay with you?"

"I'm not happy about it," Wally answered seriously, "but it'll make you happy, and you're going to make a great doctor."

"So," Phillip said, "how do we make all this happen?"

"We'll call a lawyer in the next week and start the process, if everyone agrees. And nothing can be finalized until Haven's dad's estate is settled," Dakota said with a huge smile on his face. "Now I want to stress that no one is under any obligation at this point. So talk it over and sleep on it. There's no immediate hurry."

Haven got up, still smiling, and Phillip followed behind. After saying their goodbyes, Phillip picked up his suitcase, carrying it out to the truck. "We should bring your car over to the house, too, or maybe trade it in for a real vehicle," Haven commented patting the dashboard as Phillip got in the passenger seat of the truck. "But we can do that later, I guess," Haven added as he got in.

"I had a few beers and don't think I should be driving," Phillip explained as Haven closed his door and started the engine. "So," Haven asked as he put the truck in gear, "what do you think?"

Phillip did a double take. "If it's what you want, I'm all for it."

"You don't think it's a good idea?" Haven asked, stopping the truck just before turning onto the road.

"I didn't say that. It's your ranch and your life, and I want you to be happy. I know you love being a cowboy and the other parts of owning a ranch are a little frightening for you." Phillip searched for the right words and found he was failing miserably as all the energy flowed out of Haven, and he looked miserable and unsure of himself. "Haven, let's go somewhere, and we'll talk some more." Haven turned and headed back toward the house. "Can we go to Hump Hill?"

Haven nodded, but said nothing as he drove around the range until he parked in the now-familiar space. Phillip got out and waited for Haven. Pulling down the tailgate, Phillip sat on the metal and waited for Haven to join him. The truck bounced as the younger man sat next to him. "I don't think merging the ranches is a bad idea at all." Phillip turned toward Haven and said, "I think it'll be good for you, and for Dakota and Wally. I just want to make sure you know what you're doing, because once it's done, you can't go back."

"I know, Phillip, I'm not a child."

Phillip took Haven's hand. "I never thought you were, and I didn't mean to rain on your parade, honest."

"I've thought about this for a while. It lets me be a cowboy, which is what I love, and I get to run a big ranch with thousands of head of cattle, with an experienced financial manager to back me up, along with other experienced professionals. You get a great job doing what you love too. I thought you'd be happy." Haven looked miserable, and Phillip felt like a complete shit because he was the one that had made Haven feel that way.

"I am happy, honest. I just want you to be happy as well." Phillip gathered Haven into his arms, hugging the younger man close. "I really am."

"Was that our first fight?" Haven asked a little too brightly.

"Somehow I don't think so," Phillip replied nudging Haven closer. "I'm sorry for making you feel bad. I guess I just didn't want you doing this for me."

"I'm not," Haven said softly, moving. "If I'm honest, I'm doing it for me." Their lips touched, and Phillip deepened the kiss almost immediately.

"I love it here," Phillip whispered between kisses. "You can see everything all laid out."

"It's going to be a beautiful night, clear and warm—are you up for a little camping?" Haven asked.

Phillip smiled, moving his lips close to Haven's but not quite touching. "I'd rather make love, real love, to you in our bed."

Haven shivered in the warm air, and Phillip captured his lips again, holding him close. "I love you, Haven, very much." Phillip found he wanted to say more, but didn't get the opportunity, their kisses escalating and quickly turning into a full-on make-out session. "I hate to say this, but we should get back." Haven huffed softly, but slid off the tailgate along with Phillip before slamming it back into place, getting in the truck, and heading down toward the ranch.

They didn't do much for the rest of the day. Haven rested and Phillip sat with him, knowing he'd try to do too much. After dinner, Phillip took Haven's hand and led him to the bedroom, where the covers were turned down and a single candle burned. "What's all this?"

Phillip took Haven in his arms and moved him toward the bed, his hands sliding beneath Haven's shirt, palms skimming over smooth skin. Haven's head lolled back, and Phillip took advantage, tasting the skin of his throat and neck. "Love you," Phillip whispered between licks and nips. Stripping them out of their clothes, Phillip lowered Haven onto the mattress, kissing and tasting as he listened to the sounds Haven made, those magical love noises. No rush, no hurry, Phillip made love to Haven slowly, reverently, like Haven was a temple, and Phillip took the opportunity to worship.

Haven's love music changed to small pleading sounds as Phillip prepared him with long, slow fingers and hot piercing tongue. When their bodies joined, Phillip inside Haven for the first time, Haven's heat and essence lying bare and open for him, Phillip could barely control himself. Phillip had made love to many men, but nothing prepared him for the experience of coming home. Haven was home, and Phillip swallowed hard as he realized just what he'd been missing and reveled in finally finding it. Soon, Phillip's own music joined with Haven's as well as the building accompaniment of the sounds from outside the window. Crickets, cicadas, the sounds of lowing cattle all drifted inside as though they, too, wanted to be a part of their love. "I love you, Haven," Phillip moaned softly as he felt his pleasure reaching its peak.

"Love you too, so much," Haven cried softly, as Phillip felt both their bodies clench, and with small cries of love they reached the peak of passion together.

*Chapter Thirteen*

HAVEN felt Phillip toss and turn next to him yet again. The few times he'd wakened, he'd felt Phillip tossing next to him. Looking at the windows, Haven saw only darkness, and finally Phillip seemed to settle, and Haven drifted back to sleep. Waking later, Haven found himself alone in the bed, his body stiff, the lingering soreness a reminder of their lovemaking. Slipping on his robe, Haven padded down the hall looking for Phillip, finding him sitting on the sofa, watching television, a cup of coffee in front of him on the table. "Is everything all right?" Haven asked as he walked around to the front of the sofa. "You were up for most of the night."

"I know," Phillip answered with a sigh.

"Something is wrong," Haven stated, sitting next to Phillip, taking his hand. "Just tell me."

"Yesterday, while you were meeting with Dakota, Jefferson and I had a talk. Well, it was more like Jefferson talked." Phillip turned toward Haven. "He told me what happened between him and your father."

"You. He told you? Why not me?"

"I don't know. I asked, but didn't really get a clear answer, though it seems Jefferson and your mother had an affair, of sorts," Phillip said, and Haven swallowed, not sure he really wanted to hear about this, figuring it must be bad if it had kept Phillip up all night. "She wasn't happy at home anymore, and they had a physical relationship. To be fair, Jefferson said he loved your mother, and even offered to take the heat with your dad and take care of both her and you." Phillip's speech became faster and more energetic. "When she told him she was leaving, your father flipped, and she ran to Jefferson for help, and that's how your dad found out about them." Phillip continued telling the story of what happened, and Haven tried to concentrate as his emotions and thoughts quickly became a jumbled mess.

"How could she just leave me?" Haven finally managed to ask when Phillip had finished.

"Jefferson said she meant to come back for you once she was settled," Phillip explained, and Haven saw him swallow hard.

"Does he know where she is now?" Haven asked, hope welling inside for a second until he looked in Phillip's eyes and saw his answer. "She's dead, isn't she?"

"Yes," Phillip answered.

"Oh." Haven didn't know why he was disappointed. He hadn't seen her since he was seven, but he'd always hoped. "My dad told me when she left that she didn't love us anymore and that was why she left. I never believed him because she always told me she loved me. As a kid, I couldn't figure out why she'd leave me," Haven murmured, and he heard a rustling as Phillip drew an envelope from the pocket on his robe, placing it in his hand.

"Jefferson said this arrived after she'd gone," Phillip explained, and Haven lifted the envelope, turning it over, seeing his name on the envelope. "Your mother sent that to Jefferson for you. All these years he'd kept it for you and never opened it. He asked me to give it to you."

Haven's hands shook as he ran his thumbs over the yellowed envelope, looking at Phillip and then back at the paper. He hadn't seen his mother in fourteen years. In fact, other than the pictures that hung on his wall, he had almost no recollection of her. Haven looked to Phillip for a second before slowly peeling back the sealed flap, pulling out what looked to be two pieces of letterhead paper from a hotel apparently in Las Vegas. Unfolding the sheets, Haven began to read the handwritten letter.

*My Darling Precious Boy,*

*Nothing has worked out the way I thought it would. I had hoped to find a job and a place to live so I could get you and bring you with me, but that's not possible now. More than anything in the world, I wish it were, but my life here is not what I want for you. You deserve to be happy and healthy, to grow up around horses and cattle, and to be able to play under blue skies and sleep beneath stars, things I now know I can never give you, though I want to more than life itself.*

*I know I left you and you have to be wondering why. That answer is complicated, and maybe Mr. Holden will explain things better if you ask him. You know your father and I fought all the time and we were no longer happy together, but those fights were not about you, they were about us. You were nothing but the most precious child any mother could ever ask for, and I miss you every single day.*

*There's so much I'd like to say to you, so much I wish I could be around to see, but I want you to know more than anything that I love you, I always have and I always will. Never doubt that, no matter what you think or what your father might have told you. Yes, I left, and I wish I hadn't had to, but I didn't leave you or because of you.*

*Haven, you are the light of my life and the one thing I am most proud of. So, my precious boy, please remember that I love you and always will. No matter where I am, I carry you with me next to my heart. You are never far from my thoughts.*

*My Haven, I love you always,*

*Mom.*

Haven lowered the pages to his lap, wondering what he should be feeling. "I always wondered what it was that I did that made her leave," Haven said as he handed Phillip the letter, watching as he read it.

"You didn't do anything. I think it's plain that it broke her heart to leave you." Phillip handed him back the letter, and Haven folded it, placing the pages back in the envelope. "Jefferson told me he found out a few years later that she died not long after he received this letter."

"Did he say how she died?" Haven asked, wiping his eyes with the back of his hand.

"No. He said he didn't know, and I think its best we believe him." Phillip got up from the sofa and extended his hand, leaving the coffee cup behind. "Come back to bed for a while." Haven got up as well, carrying the letter with him.

In the bedroom, Haven set the envelope against the frame of the picture of his mom and him, before stripping off the robe. Phillip curled next to him, holding him tight. "Love you, Haven," Phillip said softly, and Haven could hear his lover's breathing even out almost immediately as he began falling asleep.

"Have you thought about when you're going back to get your stuff?" Haven asked. He'd been secretly afraid for days that Phillip would change his mind and decide that he wanted to go back permanently.

"Next week. I'll make the airline reservations after I sleep a little more. Do you want to go with me?" Phillip snuggled closer.

"I can't, but I'll be waiting for you," Haven said, listening for an answer, but all he got was a soft snore as Phillip hugged him just a little tighter. Kissing Phillip's cheek, Haven closed his eyes as well. "I love you too."

*Epilogue*

PHILLIP stepped out of his office and into the autumn air, sunshine warming his skin even as the breeze held a chill, a harbinger of the cold of winter that was just around the corner. Merging the operations had been a challenge, but well worth it for everyone. "What are you doing?" Phillip called as he watched Wally working out back near his pens. Heading in that direction, he slowed his stride as he got closer to the big cats. Granted, they were securely in their cages, but a roar at close range was something he and his ears would rather not experience again.

"I need to get them ready for winter," Wally answered matter-of-factly, as he worked in Schian's pen, the lion enclosed in the exercise area, or in Schian's case today, his "nap in the sun" area. "With the cold, they need shelter, so I'm making sure Schian's is sturdy enough, and I had the guys bring over some boulders, and we'll create one for Kahn, and I need one for Blackie when she arrives next week from the Casper shelter."

"Blackie?" Phillip asked.

Wally shook his head. "She's a young black panther that someone in Casper thought would make a great pet. Unfortunately, she got out, and it took them weeks to catch her, and only after she'd hunted down every pet in the neighborhood. Like Sheba, I'm hoping I can find a zoo that will take her. She'll make a great addition to a breeding program," Wally commented as he finished up on Schian's enclosure. Closing the gate, he opened the connections to the exercise area and called Schian, who got up and ambled over, rolling on his back so Wally could rub his belly.

"Never in my life did I expect to hear a lion purr," Phillip said, staying away, but watching carefully.

"Sounds like a jet engine, doesn't he? Yes, you do, ya big baby." Wally stepped back and closed the gate, leaving Schian to bask in the sun. "I got a call from a zoo on the East Coast, and I think they might like to take Kahn, and the word seems to be out, because suddenly I'm getting lots of calls now."

"Have you heard about Sheba?"

Wally smiled as he approached. "Mom and cubs are doing just fine. The zoo in Casper is thrilled with them, and they've gotten calls about sending her to Asia on loan for breeding once the cubs are old enough," Wally explained as he opened the gates to allow Kahn into the exercise area. The regal tiger looked around before bounding into the clearing, prowling the perimeter, sniffing everything as Wally closed the gate again. "Hey, Haven," Wally called as he opened the gate, walking into the enclosure. "I've got some rocks I could use your help with."

"Sure, Wally," Haven picked up his phone, and a few minutes later three of the hands were making their way across the lawn. Haven excelled at his job, and it showed on his face almost all the time. "Hey," Haven said, turning to Phillip and planting a kiss on his mouth that threatened to melt the fencing.

"What was that for?" Phillip asked, his eyes wide.

"No reason," he answered with a wink before turning to the men. "Wally needs help with those rocks."

"Sure thing," David answered as he and the other men rolled them into place before leaning a flat rock over the top to create a cave with a small entrance on the south end.

Wally checked that it was stable and thanked the guys before shooing everyone out and closing the gate. Kahn, who'd been watching the proceedings, bounded in as soon as the gate lifted. Sniffing around the cave, he climbed all over it before venturing inside and staying there. "Now I'd say that's a hit."

"When's Dakota coming back?" Phillip asked Wally.

"This weekend. He said he'll have to study, but he's just taking refreshers now, so it's not too bad. The hard work will start for him in the spring." Wally walked around the enclosure. "I think he's anxious about leaving his dad, but Jefferson's doing really well, and the man's so proud of Dakota he could bust." It was obvious to Phillip that Wally was pretty proud of Dakota as well.

"What else do you have planned this afternoon?" Phillip asked as the group headed back toward the house.

"Nothing," Haven answered. "Why?"

"Because I thought we'd see a man about a horse. Wally said that Milford has some superb horses for sale, and I thought we'd go check them out." Haven looked at him, eyes narrowing. "It's been over six months, and you need your own horse. Your dad's is fine, but he's not yours."

Haven's scowl turned into a grin, and Phillip wondered what the man was up to. "Okay, as long as you get one too. You've been here long enough to have your own horse, so I will if you will."

Phillip huffed lightly. "Fine," he answered in mock exasperation before bursting into a smile. "I was hoping you'd say that, because Milford has one I'd like." Phillip grabbed Haven's arms and led him to the truck.

A few hours later, Phillip drove back to their house, grinning like a cat. Milford was delivering their horses the following day. Haven had gotten an almost regal chestnut gelding, and Phillip was pleased with Sahara. "Where'd you learn about horses?" Haven asked as they drove.

"I don't know anything. Why?"

"Milford said you drove the hardest bargain he'd ever seen. He said he wanted to take you with him to the yearling sales next spring."

"I guess I know how to horse trade," Phillip quipped, as Haven groaned loudly at the bad pun. "Seriously," Phillip said, shrugging, "I'm an accountant. It's my job to get the best price for everything we buy." They pulled into the yard and parked the truck. Haven gave him a quick kiss before hurrying to the barn while Phillip went in the house. Gone were the tumbledown furniture and bland walls, replaced by fresh paint, new furniture, and a complete kitchen remodel. The house felt like their home now, but it had taken a while for both of them.

Grabbing an armload of blankets from the linen closet, Phillip walked back outside, heading for the truck.

"What's that for?" Haven asked as he walked over.

"I thought we'd camp out one last time before winter," Phillip said, grunting as he heaved the blankets in the back of the truck. "There's stuff in the fridge for you to grill, and you need to put the pad for the bed in the back of the truck."

Haven's eyes grew wide. "You realize it's going to be cold tonight."

Phillip stepped close enough to smell Haven's scent and feel his breath on his lips. "Then, Mr. Heat Generator, you'll just need to keep me warm." Phillip stepped closer yet, pressing his body to Haven's, making sure his lover knew exactly what he was referring to.

Haven got the message, and very quickly the truck was packed, and they were on their way to their spot. "You know, we need to change the name of this place, because Hump Hill just doesn't cut it," Phillip said as he got out of the truck, standing on the crest of the rise looking over the land below. He could see their house as well as Wally and Dakota's, the barns, and then rangeland, unbroken rangeland. The fences that divided the ranches were now gone, the range grasses already filling in where the holes had been. "How about Phillip's Hill? That sounds much better to me."

"I bet it does," Haven said with a laugh, and Phillip tugged the man in for a kiss.

"Then how about Constellation Hill?" Phillip proposed, and Haven stopped.

"That I like," Haven whispered as he went in for another kiss that Phillip felt to his toes. "Will you point out the stars tonight?"

"If you promise to keep me warm, I'll show you anything you want," Phillip said, and Haven pressed closer.

"Is this warm enough?" Haven asked breathily as he stroked Phillip's cheek before leaning in for the kiss.

"Perfect."

Read Dakota and Wally's story in

A Shared
RANGE

ANDREW GREY

http://www.dreamspinnerpress.com

ANDREW GREY grew up in western Michigan with a father who loved to tell stories and a mother who loved to read them. Since then he has lived throughout the country and traveled throughout the world. He has a master's degree from the University of Wisconsin-Milwaukee and works in information systems for a large corporation. Andrew's hobbies include collecting antiques, gardening, and leaving his dirty dishes anywhere but in the sink (particularly when writing). He considers himself blessed with an accepting family, fantastic friends, and the world's most supportive and loving partner. Andrew currently lives in beautiful historic Carlisle, Pennsylvania.

Visit Andrew's web site at http://www.andrewgreybooks.com and blog at http://andrewgreybooks.livejournal.com/. E-mail him at andrewgrey @comcast.net.

Contemporary Romance by ANDREW GREY

# Also by ANDREW GREY

http://www.dreamspinnerpress.com

# Contemporary Fantasy by ANDREW GREY

www.ingramcontent.com/pod-product-compliance
Lightning Source LLC
Chambersburg PA
CBHW070017260626

47159CB00005B/1841